W9-AYH-317

Lake of Secrets

Lake

of

Secrets

lael littke

 NICHOLS MIDDLE SCHOOL
800 GREENLEAF STREET
EVANSTON, IL 60202

Henry Holt and Company

New York

Henry Holt and Company, LLC, *Publishers since 1866*
115 West 18th Street, New York, New York 10011
www.henryholt.com

Henry Holt is a registered trademark of Henry Holt and Company, LLC
Distributed in Canada by H. B. Fenn and Company Ltd.

Library of Congress Cataloging-in-Publication Data
Littke, Lael.
Lake of secrets / Lael Littke.
p.   cm.
Summary: Having arrived in her mother's hometown to try to find her long-missing brother,
who disappeared three years before she was born, fifteen-year-old Carlene
finds herself haunted by memories from a past life.
[1. Reincarnation—Fiction.   2. Missing persons—Fiction.
3. Mystery and detective stories.]   I. Title.
PZ7.L719 Lak 2002   [Fic]—dc21   2001039933

ISBN 0-8050-6730-2 / First Edition—2002
Printed in the United States of America on acid-free paper. ∞
1 3 5 7 9 10 8 6 4 2

For Ernie and Patty,

whose friendship warms my life,

and for Walter,

who so generously shares his time and knowledge

Lake of Secrets

one

There is always this: Families are forever.

For as long as I can remember, that needlepoint saying has been the first thing I've seen whenever I walk through Grandma's front door. It's there in her entry hall along with faded photographs of our relatives. It's right where you can't avoid looking at it, unless you glue your eyes to the floor.

Grandma believes it. "Families are forever," she says, even though most of those relatives on the wall are dead and gone. Even though my brother, Keith, disappeared eighteen years ago, three years before I was born, and nobody had ever found out what happened to him. "Keith is still your brother," Grandma says. "Wherever he is, alive or dead, he's your brother."

"Keith is alive," my mom always declares.

Then there's my dad. "He's still your father,"

Grandma says, "no matter what he did. Always will be. Forever."

Even though he dumped Mom and me at Grandma's house when I was nine and left for somewhere else, as out of reach as Keith.

He left *because* of Keith. Because Mom couldn't give Keith up, couldn't let go of him, couldn't stop sending out *MISSING* flyers and putting his picture on milk cartons even after she had to have them computer-enhanced to show what he'd look like as he got older. He was only four years old when he disappeared.

Mom couldn't be happy with just me and Dad. We weren't enough. She had to find out what happened to Keith.

And that's why she and I were moving back to Lake Isadora where he disappeared all those years ago.

The memory came as soon as I saw the valley with what was left of the lake sparkling like a sapphire in its center. After six years of drought, the man-made lake had receded so far that some of the foundations of the buildings that had once been there in the valley were visible again, after being underwater for a long time. We couldn't see the foundations from where we were, but Mom had read about them in the Lake Isadora newspaper she still subscribed to.

She'd also read a short article on the back page of the

same issue about some child's clothing being found in an old abandoned mine shaft nearby. Mom was sure the clothing was Keith's. But that wasn't what the memory was about.

The impression that built itself in my mind as I looked at the valley was of Jonathan. He stood in the doorway of the small ice cream store where we liked to go for triple-deckers, that narrow little shop with the stale, sunbaked candy in its front window. I saw Jonathan's smile and heard his quick laughter, but as he reached out to hand something to me the memory was gone, as if somebody had hit the off button on a TV remote control.

"It's pretty, isn't it?" Mom broke into my thoughts. "The valley, I mean. I can't believe the lake has shrunk down to practically nothing. It was once so big. And treacherous."

Her voice faded, as if she were musing to herself. She'd stopped the car and turned off the engine as we crested the hill. She said she wanted to get a good look from up there on the summit. She wanted to ease herself back into this place where the terrible thing had happened. Where Keith had gone missing. The old newspaper articles in Mom's scrapbook said that he was presumed to have drowned during a violent storm on the lake. He and his dad—*my* dad, too—had been out in a boat.

I felt disoriented as I looked down at the valley

because I didn't know where the impression of Jonathan came from. Had it been hiding in some crevice of my brain, buried under Mom's constant talk of Keith? For how long? Was it the sight of the lake that released the unexpected memory?

I didn't remember the lake, which disoriented me even more. Where was the town? Where was the ice cream shop that had been so clear in my mind?

Chilly fingers of panic slid down my spine. It was like when you're overtired and fall asleep in the afternoon, then awaken not knowing where you are, what time it is, who might be there with you.

I took a deep breath. Of course I knew where the town was. Mom had told me all about the high earthen dam I could see in the distance. She'd said the buildings of the town—all the houses and stores and the old hotel—had been moved to higher ground before the valley floor was flooded. The river had been dammed to create a lake that would supply irrigation water for the broad agricultural plain we'd passed through half an hour earlier and also prevent the devastating floods that frequently occurred in the spring.

But now the drought had made the waters shrink down to what appeared, from where we were, to be an enormous pond.

"I have something for you, Carlene," Mom said. Her voice sounded far away. "A gift for your fifteenth birthday. I wanted to give it to you here, just as we got our first glimpse of the lake."

She reached behind the seat and brought out a brightly wrapped package. I hadn't noticed it before because it was buried in the back seat of the car in the midst of almost everything we owned, which wasn't much.

"Open it," Mom said, handing the package to me.

Carefully I undid the well-worn blue ribbon and folded back the wrapping paper. It was the red geranium paper, wrinkled and creased and soft with age. How many times had it been recycled now? It bugged me the way Mom kept using things until they literally fell apart.

"We're doing it to save money," she always said. "So we can find Keith."

I wanted to rip the paper from the package, tear it to bits, and toss it in the garbage sack by my feet, along with the old banana peels and empty pop cans. I wanted to tell Mom to forget this useless quest of hers and take me back to Arletta where my friends were. Where my life was.

But that would bring on a "yeller," which is what Mom calls our arguments. This wasn't a good time for one. We'd had the grandmother of all yellers two weeks before when Mom had told me we were moving. I hadn't wanted to go, even for Keith.

Or maybe because it *was* for Keith. I'd lived in his

7

shadow my entire life. Perfect Keith, my "families-are-forever" lost brother.

But I pushed all thoughts of him aside. I'd have to deal with that soon enough.

"Like it?" Mom asked as I lifted the lid off the box.

"The wrapping paper? Yes, I've always liked it. It's been one of my favorites for years and years and years."

I knew Mom wasn't talking about the paper, but I said it anyway.

Mom sighed. "Carlene, must you be so obtuse?"

Obtuse.

Mom was a walking dictionary. That was another item on my things-that-bug-me list.

I examined my fingernails as I considered various answers. I'd painted my nails in red and white stripes with a tiny blue star in the center of each one for the Fourth of July. I liked them that way and hadn't peeled the polish off even though it was now the middle of the month.

I could say, "Obtuse. Rhymes with goose. Noose. Caboose."

Depending on Mom's mood, she might come back with, "And moose. And truce." Then we'd be off on a game.

On the other hand, it was hot and Mom had been driving for five hours already that day, and for longer than that the day before. Her blond hair, so like my own, hung limp and damp against her neck, and she looked tired. She was tense, too, now that we were back to the place where Keith had disappeared so long ago. He'd be twenty-two now, if he was alive.

I didn't try for the word game. I had the feeling that if I got too cute right now Mom would call me a smart-mouth and then of course I'd start yelling about that and we'd be off again.

So I settled for saying, "Now looking inside box. Pushing aside tissue paper. Seeing . . . oh!" I'd thought it would be something trivial and flimsy, the way my birthday gifts always were. But it wasn't.

"Binoculars!" I didn't have to make an effort to sound enthusiastic.

Mom smiled, obviously pleased that I liked my gift. "They're quite powerful. I picked them up at a garage sale."

I felt a tweak of resentment. Why couldn't she have kept to herself the fact that the binoculars were some-body else's castoff, like almost everything else we owned?

But then I was ashamed. Mom did the best she could. She'd kept us going ever since my dad left. We'd had to live with Grandma, whose one-bedroom apart-ment was not big enough for all of us. Mom had slept on the living room sofa, and I'd had a cot in the service porch, snug up against the dryer. Mom worked as a substitute teacher, which didn't bring in a whole lot, but it had been okay. At least I'd had friends there in Arletta—my best friend, Dawnelle, and others who didn't even know about Keith. My biggest desire was to go back there as soon as Mom got her mind settled about those clothes that had been found in the mine.

I understood, or at least I tried to understand, why she'd saved every spare penny for the time when we could come here to Lake Isadora to look for Keith. She was convinced that he hadn't drowned on that day so long ago, that somebody had just taken him. All we had to do was spend the time and money to find him.

I picked up the glasses. Inexperienced though I was, I could tell they'd been expensive when new. Mom could never have afforded anything that good, except at a garage sale.

"They're great, Mom," I said. "I'll have fun with these." I raised them to my eyes so I could look at the lake.

"I thought they could be helpful in looking for clues," Mom said.

I might have known Keith would be involved even in my birthday present. But how ridiculous it was to think we'd find clues after eighteen years.

"Look over that way." Mom raised a hand to point. "See that outcropping of rocks?"

I peered through the glasses. "Where? I don't see it."

Mom reached over to turn my head slightly. "Look at the right side of the lake. See the tall pines back a little bit from the water?"

I nodded.

"There's a cabin there. Can you see it?"

"Is that where you lived?" I asked.

"No. That was Perla Goudy's cabin. Probably still is. Now follow the edge of the lake to the left, then pull back toward the hill. You should see the outcropping of rocks."

I did. "Got it," I said.

"That used to be a major landmark, before the valley was flooded," Mom said. "The house where I was born was just down the street from those rocks. About a block from the school, which was right in front of the rocks."

Once again Jonathan flashed into my memory. Jonathan, and the yellow brick schoolhouse. It had been two stories, with tall, many-paned windows. It had been both elementary and high school, with four classrooms downstairs and four upstairs, each with a blackboard on an inside wall and a picture of George Washington behind the teacher's desk.

There'd been an apple tree beside the school. I could almost taste the tartness of those apples that hung red and rosy, like ornaments, each September, soon after the school term began. I remembered Jonathan handing one of them to me, and how the juice ran down my chin as I bit into it.

But then the scene faded, as swiftly and completely as the first memory had gone.

Again I felt disoriented. Although he seemed totally real in those flashes, I couldn't locate Jonathan in my memory bank. Who was he?

"Mom," I said. "Who's Jonathan?"

She glanced at me. "You mean Jonathan Petersen? Back in Arletta?"

Starting the car, she headed it down the hill toward the lake.

"No," I said. "Jonathan here in Lake Isadora."

Her forehead furrowed. "Jonathan? The only Jonathan I can think of here is Jonathan Winward. He was one of my teachers at school."

I wouldn't be remembering one of my mother's schoolteachers as a friend of mine. So the Jonathan I was thinking of had to be a little boy I'd met when we'd visited here back before I could remember.

On the other hand, I must have been in school, because the classrooms and the apple tree were clear in my mind. But I'd gone to kindergarten and the early grades back in Chalmers where we'd lived when Dad was with us. When he left and we moved in with Grandma in Arletta, I'd gone to school there. I'd never been in school here in Lake Isadora. Yet in those memory fragments I was old enough to go with Jonathan to the ice cream parlor. Old enough to be pleased when he gave me an apple from the tree by the school. The tree and school that were no longer there.

Uneasily I lowered the binoculars. "Mom," I said. "When did they build the dam here and flood the valley?"

She tapped the steering wheel with a forefinger as she thought. "Well, let's see, I was fourteen when our house was moved. I'm forty-two now. How's your arithmetic?"

It was good enough to figure out that the lake had been there for close to thirty years. The schoolhouse and the apple tree and the ice cream shop had been gone for at least that long.

I was fifteen.

My mind scurried to find an explanation. Well, sure, we must have come back for a summer when I was little. I was remembering the new town, the one where the old buildings had been taken to higher ground.

But why then was the outcropping of rocks so familiar?

My throat was desert-dry as I said, "Mom, when was I last here?"

Mom glanced briefly at me as she drove down the narrow road leading to Lake Isadora. "You've never been here before, Carlene," she said. "Never in your whole life."

two

The town of Lake Isadora was small. There wasn't really a main street, or at least not one like you generally think of in the central part of a town. There were stores, but they seemed to be casually left wherever their owners had set them down when the old town was moved to make way for the lake. The whole place looked as if it had just happened, without much planning.

I was relieved that nothing seemed familiar. Not the school, which was beige stucco, instead of yellow brick like the one I remembered. Not the rustic little motel where Mom and I checked in. And not the small newspaper office, which was the first place we headed after cleaning up at the motel.

I hadn't told Mom about my strange memories. What was the point? She'd say I'd seen pictures of the old yellow schoolhouse in her photo albums. She might even say I was just imagining those scenes so she'd abandon the search for Keith and take me back home. She was tired of hearing how much I missed Dawnelle and my other friends.

Besides, there didn't seem to be any more of the memories, so why stir up new problems when there were already more than I could handle? Maybe I'd just been too hot in the car, since it didn't have air conditioning. Maybe I'd been hallucinating or something.

The newspaper office was on an alleylike side street that went off at an angle to the highway. It was between a hardware store and a small café named Ivy's Eats. *Lake Isadora Citizen* was printed on the glass door of the office. A bell jingled as we opened the door and went inside.

The small room seemed crowded, with a cluttered desk, a water cooler, and a couple of chairs next to a small table adorned with a plant. There was a waist-high counter that barred access to an archway that I assumed led to offices and a print shop, or a photo lab, or whatever was needed to put out a newspaper.

Mom looked around. "It's just like it used to be," she said. "Complete with dying fern." She pointed at the dusty plant that looked as if it needed water. "I wonder if it's the same one."

For a moment I was startled. Sometimes I forgot that Mom had had a life before I was born. She'd lived here and had probably been to this newspaper office many times. All these things were stored in her memory—that's why she'd known exactly where to turn to get to the motel, and why she'd known where this office was. She'd grown up in this town and had even seen it moved from its original location, now under the lake.

Why, then, didn't she remember Jonathan?

Why did I?

A woman came through one of the doors in the hallway and hurried toward us. "Sorry," she said breathlessly. "Our receptionist is off doing some library research. We all have double duty here. Now, what can—" She stopped, peering at Mom. "Jen, is that you?"

"It's me, Mariah," Mom said with a big grin. "I wondered how long it would take you to recognize me."

Mariah raised a little shelf in the counter and practically leaped through the opening. "For heaven's sake," she said, throwing her arms around Mom. "It's been a hundred years since I last saw you."

"At least," Mom said. They hugged hard, then stepped apart, looking at each other. "You haven't changed much since we were in school. Don't people here get old like the rest of us?"

"Too busy for that," Mariah said. She turned to me. "This has to be your daughter. Looks just like your boy." She stopped, putting a hand to her mouth. "Oh,

17

wow, I'm always chewing on my foot. I'm sorry, Jen. I shouldn't have said that. I just remember that he was fair-haired and blue-eyed with cheeks like ripe peaches. Same as—" She smiled at me.

"Carlene," Mom said. "We named her after Carl."

Carl. My dad. My families-are-forever-but-not-necessarily-together dad.

Mariah hugged me. "Delighted to know you, Carlene." She didn't ask anything about my dad. I guess she already knew he and Mom had split. Turning to Mom, she said, "Sorry I got off to a bad start."

"It's okay," Mom said evenly. "It's been a long time." She put a hand on my arm. "Carlene, this is Mariah. She was queen of everything when we were in high school. Homecoming and rodeo and even Miss Mining Days. Everything."

Mariah leaned close to me. "I was Cleopatra, too, in a past life," she fake-whispered.

I liked Mariah. She had black hair and black-fringed deep-blue eyes and black smudges on her face. Printer's ink, I assumed. On her, even that was attractive.

I didn't know what to say to a celebrity, a queen. A former Cleopatra.

"Do you work here?" I said finally.

"Oh, yes," she confided. "Elizabeth II seems to be the only one who makes a profit at queening. I had to find something else to do."

She and Mom hooted together, and because I was so happy to see my mom laugh, I laughed, too.

"That's better, Carlene," Mariah said. "You seemed kind of serious up till now."

"Mariah is the editor, " Mom said. "Didn't you see it on the door?"

I turned to look at the door. A young guy was walking past. He raised a hand in greeting, and for a moment I thought he was waving at me. But then Mariah waved back, saying, "That's my son. Looks just like his dad, doesn't he?"

"How *is* Stan? Still tossing a football?" Mom asked, and they were off on a tour of old times.

I walked over to examine the printing on the door. From inside it was backward, but I could see that it said "Mariah Kelsey, Publisher and Editor."

Just to have something to do, I went to the cooler and filled a cup with water. After drinking part of it, I poured the rest into the limp fern.

There was a book on the table by the plant. Picking it up, I read the title: *Buried in Water: A History of a Drowned Town*. The jacket picture was of the yellow brick schoolhouse, with the outcropping of rocks on the hillside behind.

Quickly I put the book down. My heart thudded so loud that I thought Mom and Mariah must hear it.

Surely Mom had a photo like that. Somewhere in

those albums of hers I *must* have seen it, the schoolhouse and the apple tree and the rocks in the background.

Then why did I taste the tartness of the apples? Why did I see the jutting-jawed portrait of George Washington hanging on the wall in back of the teacher's desk, a battered golden-oak desk with the initials A.D. scratched on one leg?

Behind me Mariah was saying, "There are still several familiar faces around here. Neil McCrae and Belle. Arty Blair. Sylvia. And guess who I saw on the street the other day? Remember Davy Van Dyke?"

Mom's eyebrows raised. "Davy? I thought he was in prison."

Prison? Apparently this wasn't a totally sleepy little town.

Mariah dismissed Davy with a shrug. "We should have a party with some of our school friends. How long will you be here?"

"As long as it takes," Mom said.

There was a small silence, then Mariah said, "Uh— excuse me? Did I miss something?"

"I came to find Keith," Mom said in a bright, upbeat voice, as if it were merely a problem of looking around until she spotted him. "That article in the *Citizen* a while ago about the stuff found in the mine—I'm sure the child's clothing is Keith's."

I turned around to see Mariah put on what I used to call a "sorry face." It was the face people wore when they talked about Keith.

"Oh, Jen," she said. "Oh, Jen."

"Who has the stuff?" Mom asked blandly. "Where can I see it?"

"I suppose Bud Brady has it," Mariah said. "Remember him? He's the long arm of the law around here now." She touched Mom's shoulder. "It's such a long shot, Jen. Are you sure you want to stir all that up again?"

Mom nodded jerkily. "I need to know."

"I think I'll go explore the town," I said in a hoarse-sounding voice.

I didn't want to be there when Mom went over the details, how she'd always felt that Keith was alive, how she'd saved for years to return and hire someone to track down anybody who might have been at the lake the day he disappeared, how she'd had this *feeling* when she read the article about the stuff in the mine. I didn't want to be there when the brightness in her voice faded and she began to cry yet again about my lost brother.

Mariah turned to look at me. "Okay, sweetie," she said. "But there's not much to see. You might want to check out the museum and see how the old town looked when your mom and I were little kids. Just turn right for two blocks and hang a left. You can't miss it."

"Okay," I said, knowing I wasn't going to the museum.

"Stop in at the ice cream shop," Mariah said. "Best cones in the West."

"Okay," I said again. I turned toward the door, knowing I wasn't going anywhere near any ice cream shop either. What if it was the same one as in my memory? What if Jonathan was there, holding out a cone to me? Whoever Jonathan was.

"Wait." Mariah walked back through the opening in the counter. "I know somebody who'd like to show a pretty girl like you around. Protect you from rattlesnakes and all that." Poking her head through the archway, she called, "J.P., are you still here?"

J.P. Was he the one who'd passed the door a while ago, Mariah's son?

I didn't want to meet him. I was too full of strange emotions right then to have to smile and giggle and be charming to a guy.

"Wait," I said, but it was too late. I heard soft footsteps coming down the hall. I couldn't see who it was until he came out into the room because his head, with its buzz-cut blond hair, wasn't as high as the counter.

"Hi," he said. "What's up?"

He wore a pair of light-colored shorts and a neatly

knotted necktie. His chest was bare, except for the tie, and so were his feet.

"J.P.," Mariah said, "I'd like you to meet Carlene and her mother, Mrs. Carter." To us she said, "This is J.P. He's seven." She winked at me and I knew she knew I would have been uneasy about meeting an older guy right at that moment.

J.P. offered an ink-stained hand. "Pleased to meetchoo," he said politely. "Watch out for the wart. It's yucky to touch." He pointed to a craggy lump on his thumb, which he held upright as he shook hands with us.

"Nice to meet you, too, J.P.," Mom said. "I guess your mother keeps you busy here."

J.P. looked puzzled.

"I'm not his mother," Mariah said, "although I'd like to claim him." She put an arm around J.P.'s bare shoulders. "J.P.'s the local pet. He works wherever he's needed. And right now, J.P., we need you to show Carlene around town."

J.P. grinned, showing big, new front teeth. "Come on, Carlene." He took me by the hand and led me out into the hot mountain air.

Looking at the town with J.P. was like seeing the world with new eyes. Alone, I never would have noticed the bird's nest in the pyracantha hedge. ("How does the mother bird get in there without slicing herself on the thorns?" he asked.) I wouldn't have talked to the gray-haired woman bent over a walker. ("Does your leg feel any better today, Mrs. Gilly?" J.P. inquired.)

I wouldn't have seen the half-finished house behind the cedar trees on top of the hill. ("All the up-and-down boards are there, like a skeleton.") Nor would I have gotten acquainted with the lonely dog chained to the fence enclosing a junkyard. ("I take him for walks when Mr. Finney lets me.") I wouldn't even have noticed that one of my star-spangled fingernails had only three stripes while all the others had four. ("Do you have stars on your toenails, too, Carlene?")

I wondered, as I listened to J.P., if Keith would have been anything like him, and for the first time in my life I thought I might really have liked my brother. Of course he would have been a lot older. A big brother. He probably would have defended me when other kids teased me, and told me silly knock-knock jokes.

"Knock knock," I said.

J.P. looked up at me, grinning. "Who's there?"

"Candy."

"Candy who?"

"Candy cow jump over de moon?"

J.P. giggled. "That's funny, Carlene," he said. "I like you."

"I like you, too," I told him. "You make me think of my brother." I smiled down at him, noticing again the odd fact that he wore a necktie against his bare chest. "Hey, pal, what's the necktie for? Is today a special occasion or something?"

Suddenly J.P. was very quiet. He looked at me with shadowed eyes, then asked, "What's your brother's name?"

Okay. So J.P.'s life was not totally uncomplicated either. I'd have to remember not to trespass in that territory again.

"His name is Keith," I said.

"Is he nice?"

"I don't know. I've never met him. He's lost."

J.P. considered that. "Have you looked for him on the computer? My aunt Fran is always looking for my mom on the computer."

So his mother was gone. I filed that information away. "I've never tried looking for him on the computer. How does your aunt Fran do it?"

"Want to go ask her? She works at the library."

"Sure," I said. What could it hurt? I probably wouldn't find out anything about Keith, but I might learn more about J.P.

"The library's around the corner," J.P. said, turning left.

I followed him, and suddenly I was caught in a nightmare because there was the library, the little library that I knew so well, with its smell of glue and old books and the vines that grew along its brown walls almost covering the windows, so that when you sat at one of the dark, heavy tables it seemed as if you were inside a tree house. And Jonathan was there standing in the doorway.

three

"Jonathan!" I whispered.

J.P. looked at me curiously, then glanced toward the library. "That guy? That's not Jonathan. That's Luke. He plays football."

It *wasn't* Jonathan.

I could see that now. He was taller and his hair was lighter and longer than Jonathan ever wore his. Jonathan's hair was dark. "Axle-grease black," he used to say.

My stomach lurched, and for a moment I thought I would be sick. Where were these memories coming from? It was like when telephone wires get crossed and you listen in on somebody else's conversation. I was tapping into somebody else's memory bank. What other explanation could there be?

"Jonathan lives up on the mountain in that house

that looks like a skeleton." J.P. pointed up to the half-finished house on the hill. "He doesn't come to town much. Only to get groceries."

J.P. pronounced it "grosh'ries,"and I tried to focus on that. Tried to ignore that there really *was* a Jonathan living in Lake Isadora. Did he have axle-grease black hair? Would I know him if I saw him?

"He's an old guy," J.P. said.

"Old? How old?"

J.P. shrugged. "Real old."

I didn't pursue it. To a kid like J.P., old could mean anybody over eighteen. But this Jonathan could be the same one Mom remembered, the one who'd been her schoolteacher.

I took a deep breath, squashing the memory of Jonathan down somewhere but knowing it wouldn't stay there. "Hey, pal," I said to J.P., "what say we go visit that computer?"

There was one problem. We had to pass Luke, who still stood in the doorway as if he were waiting for someone. He grinned when J.P. waved a hand and said, "Hi, Luke."

"Hi, yourself," Luke said. "Who's your friend?"

His grin, big and toothy, included me. He was like a friendly puppy, sure that I would respond to him.

I did.

Not that I wanted to. I didn't want to get involved

28

with him any more than I'd wanted to get acquainted with Mariah's son back at the newspaper office. But he reminded me of Jonathan. There was no way I could ignore it. I didn't even know *why* he reminded me of Jonathan. How could I when I didn't know *who* Jonathan was?

"It's Carlene," J.P. said to Luke. "She knows knock-knock jokes."

"Knock knock," Luke said.

"Who's there?" I answered automatically.

"Aw, you've already heard it," Luke said.

J.P. giggled, a joyous, happy sound that made me giggle, too.

A girl came from the dimness of the library carrying a stack of books, a girl whose dark eyes said "No trespassing" when she saw me there beside Luke. Linking her arm with his, she whisked him away without even acknowledging me, except for that single look.

As they left, Luke turned and grinned like the Cheshire cat, then was gone.

"That's Angelique," J.P. informed me. "That girl."

The library was old and scruffy and as cozy as a well-loved chair by the fireplace. Even though I'd had that flash of recognition when I'd first seen it, I felt nothing other than its friendliness when we went inside.

I touched one of the sturdy dark tables as I passed,

noting that its surface was scarred with carved initials. I stopped to run my fingers over one set that was deeper than the others: RP + TC. For some reason I was relieved that I saw no J's. J for Jonathan.

A voice spoke beside me. "People like to leave evidence that they were here."

"Hi, Aunt Fran," J.P. said. "This is my friend Carlene."

J.P.'s aunt was a lot younger than I'd figured she'd be. Twenty-something, I guessed. She had blond hair like his and was just a bit overweight.

Putting out her hand, she said, "Any friend of J.P.'s is a friend of mine." She seemed as comfortable and easy to like as the old books on the shelves. She was immediately interested in my problem when J.P. told her I was looking for my lost brother.

"We'll do a looky-loo on the Web," she said, scooping a stack of books from the table and heading toward the main desk. "Amazing what clues you can find there." She stashed the books on a cart, checked out some other books for a waiting patron, then led J.P. and me into a small room that seemed full of computers. Sitting down in front of one, she motioned for us to pull up chairs. "I'm sorry to hear that your brother is lost," she said. "How did it happen? Did he run away or something?"

J.P. looked up at me. "My mom ran away. When

I was little. She hasn't come back yet." As he spoke, he stroked the necktie that hung down across his bare chest.

Well, so much for Grandma's thing about "families are forever." With some families it didn't apply. You couldn't be a forever family if your mother left you when you were scarcely old enough to remember her. You couldn't be a forever family if your mom was so hung up on your dead brother that she didn't even notice that other members of the family, alive and right there in front of her eyes, needed a little attention, too.

"She was in Denver last time I located her on the Web," Fran said. "Used to be in Ohio. Seems to be moving back toward California a little at a time."

I realized she was talking about J.P.'s mother. "You mean you can find her?" I asked. "On the computer, I mean?"

"Sometimes. But that doesn't mean I can get in touch with her. Or make her get in touch with us." Fran's hands moved over the keyboard. "Any idea as to what part of the country your brother might be in?"

Could it be *that* easy? Just click the mouse a few times and Keith's whereabouts would show up on the computer screen? Of course Mom would then insist that we rush off to wherever he was. This was the whole reason we had come back to Lake Isadora, right? We'd be off again before we even unpacked the car.

Maybe it would be a good thing. Maybe I could leave behind all the strange memories that weren't really memories.

And the sooner we found Keith, the sooner I could go back to my friends.

"No," I said to Fran. "I don't have a clue as to where he might be."

Fran was still touching the keyboard and clicking the mouse. The computer hummed and lights on the modem flashed. "Makes it harder," she said. "What's his name?"

"Keith Carter. I don't even know if he's still alive," I confessed. "Maybe he drowned in the lake eighteen years ago."

Fran sat back in her chair. "Oh," she said. "You're Keith Carter's sister."

I nodded.

"I was in the fourth grade when he disappeared," Fran said. "I remember it really well. Why didn't you say right off that you were looking for Keith Carter?"

I couldn't help but feel a little startled. Being here, meeting Mariah and Fran who had both known Keith, was like finding out that a fictional character you'd read about when you were a little kid was, in fact, quite real. Here were people besides my family who had known Keith. He still existed, not only in the memories of my family but in Fran's mind, too, and in Mariah's.

J.P. peered at the computer screen. "Can you find him, Aunt Fran?" he asked.

Fran slowly shook her head. "I don't know, honeybun."

"My mom thinks maybe somebody took him," I said.

"If they did, they probably changed his name," Fran said. "We don't know what name to look for."

"Try," J.P. said. He was young enough to still believe in magic.

Fran clicked the mouse to bring up more stuff on the screen, then typed "Keith Carter" on the line where the cursor pulsed.

The red lights on the modem flickered busily. It took quite a while for anything to happen, but eventually some writing and a picture began to form on the screen. I leaned closer, peering at it.

My heart thudded. Maybe there really was magic in the world.

But what came up on the screen was one of the flyers my mom had sent out a couple of years before. "Have you seen this boy?" it said beside a computer-enhanced picture to show what Keith might have looked like then.

The computer wasn't finished. Another picture was forming. It was of Keith at age four, the preschool photo my mom kept on her bedside table.

As I stared at the screen, I felt queasy again because I had a distinct memory of Keith. Of *Keith*, who disappeared, or died, three years before I was born.

He was in a boat with another person, and I was looking at him from somewhere else.

And Jonathan was by my side.

four

It occurred to me that if I were a house, I would be haunted, what with Jonathan hanging around the way he did.

The thought made me smile, and that was comforting. I wasn't too far over the edge if I could still think things were funny.

Besides, there had to be some simple explanation for these things that were happening to me. Fran's comfortable presence made everything seem so very normal.

I took a couple of deep breaths as I watched Keith's image brighten on the screen.

Fran must have heard because she said, "I know this can't be easy for you, Carlene. Even if you never knew Keith."

She reached over to squeeze my hand.

J.P. hitched his chair closer to me, gazing at the picture of the boy on the monitor screen. "Is that your lost brother?"

"Yes," I said.

J.P. squinted at the picture. "He's *little*. Littler than me. How'd he get lost?"

"I don't know." I was surprised that my breath caught in my throat. Before now, Keith had been merely an irritation to me, the perfect sibling who could do no wrong because he wasn't there. He'd been the yardstick against which I'd been measured all my life. Never whiny, never obstreperous (another of Mom's dictionary words).

I guess it was J.P.'s presence that made Keith seem suddenly real. He had been a little boy once, too. Warm and friendly and curious about everything around him. He hadn't really been perfect, any more than J.P. was perfect. I would have liked him, as I liked J.P.

I would have *loved* him, because he was my brother.

An image of him formed in my mind. He was dressed in striped overalls and a red plaid shirt and wore a billed cap. He stood on the shore of the lake, and as I came toward him he turned to smile and show me what he had in the small red bucket he carried.

The image faded before I saw what was in the bucket.

There had probably been a picture in one of Mom's

albums of Keith on the shore of the lake dressed in striped overalls. Or maybe in the box of photos Grandma kept on a little table in her living room.

Somewhere I must have seen that picture. That's why it had come into my mind.

"Yes, he was littler than you, J.P.," Fran said. "I'll tell you about him." Leaning back in her chair she said, "I might be able to find an old news report of it on the computer. Or I can just tell it."

"Tell it," I said. That seemed closer, more personal.

Fran nodded. "I was only ten," she said. "I'm looking at it through a ten-year-old's eyes. And it was eighteen years ago, remember."

"How well did you know him?" I asked.

"Not well," Fran admitted. "I saw him around town with your folks. But how much attention does a ten-year-old pay to little kids who aren't relatives or neighbors? I saw him occasionally on the street, since this isn't a very large town. Mainly I just remember when he disappeared. You're not apt to forget that kind of thing, even if you're only ten." She paused, staring at me. "He looked a lot like you, Carlene."

"That's what Mariah said."

Fran's eyebrows went up. "You've met Mariah."

I nodded. "She and my mom were friends in high school."

"Oh," Fran said.

There was a lot loaded into that "Oh." Maybe sometime later I'd find out more about what baggage was there, but now didn't seem to be the time. For one thing, Fran wasn't likely to say much in front of J.P. For another, I was anxious to hear her version of what had happened to Keith. My ghost brother, who looked like me.

J.P. was getting restless. "What happened to Keith?" he asked. "How old was he?"

Fran put an arm around his shoulders. "He was four. Littler than you, like you said, J.P." Her voice dropped to the soft, confidential level of a storyteller. "It was on a hot Saturday in early July."

She might well have said "Once upon a time," because the reality of Keith that I'd felt a few minutes before now faded into fairy tale again as I listened to the familiar story. Mom gone shopping in town. Keith and Dad deciding to go to the lake. The two of them out in a boat. A sudden thunderstorm, with high winds. The boat overturned in rough water. Dad trapped under the boat, but eventually rescued, half-drowned. The frantic efforts of everybody in town to find Keith. The hideous task of telling Mom. The way she stood on the shore, calling his name out over the choppy waters.

Fran was right; she hadn't forgotten anything about the day, even though she'd been so young at the time.

"We never found anything," she said. "They dragged the lake for days, but nobody ever found a clue to what happened to him."

J.P. let out a deep breath, as if he'd been holding it.

"Mom thinks those clothes that were found in the old mine might have been Keith's," I said.

Fran's eyes widened. "I wonder if they could be. I remember your mother wasn't sure what he'd been wearing, because she wasn't there when he got dressed to go to the lake."

"And Dad couldn't remember, after he almost drowned. Besides, he's color-blind."

So many times I had heard them go over those facts. So many arguments had stalled on the fact that Dad couldn't even remember what Keith was wearing at the time. And Mom couldn't figure out exactly which clothes were missing from his closet, because Keith was forever stashing clothes in odd places and pulling them out later to wear.

"I wonder if Jonathan might remember if he saw them," Fran said.

The name sent a jolt through me, as if I'd stuck my finger into a live light socket.

"Jonathan?" It came out not much more than a whisper.

"Jonathan Winward," Fran said. "He saw your dad and Keith out in their boat right before the water got really rough. He was injured somehow in the accident. His wife was drowned."

"Oh, no," I said. But my mind snagged on the fact that there *was* a Jonathan present that day. I'd probably seen the name in one of the old newspaper articles. And I knew the story so well that I just put myself into it with him. He must be the Jonathan in my memories.

"This Jonathan, how old is he?" I asked.

Fran looked at me curiously. "I don't know. Somewhere around sixty, I'd guess."

A door slammed in my mind, locking Jonathan out. I didn't want to know any more about him. The memories I'd had were of a young Jonathan, someone my own age.

"He lives up on the hill," J.P. said. "In that house that's not finished."

So he was the same Jonathan J.P. had mentioned earlier. And probably Mom's old schoolteacher, as I'd concluded before.

I didn't want to meet him.

And I didn't want to hear any more about Keith. I had a life. I wanted to think about something else.

Leaning back in my chair, I fake yawned. "How's the junk food here in Lake Isadora? I didn't have much breakfast."

Fran grinned. "Ivy's Eats does a great burger," she said. "I'll spring for lunch for all three of us."

"Oh, hey," I said, "I wasn't hinting. I just—"

"Forget the protests." Fran stood up. "The treat's on me. Come on, I'm hungry."

"Me, too," J.P. said.

Fran was right. Ivy's Eats did put out a great burger, with all the trimmings. And fries the likes of which I'd never tasted before. All cooked by Ivy herself, who talked nonstop while she presided over the spotless grill.

We learned that there'd been a loud argument between Howard and Ellen in front of the movie theater the night before. The high school English teacher had gotten a speeding ticket. Avery Hubbard's barking dog had inspired Thelma Whipple to call the police. And Luke and Angelique had been there in the café for lunch just before we came.

"That Angelique," Ivy declared. "Blind as a post when it comes to how to handle the likes of Luke. She's carryin' on and sheddin' tears big as a fist, just because he said howdy to another gal. She oughta cut him a little slack, him bein' a young guy needin' to wear out a coupla saddles before he picks a corral."

Translated, I figured that meant things weren't too cozy between Luke and Angelique after all. . . .

Which was a good thing to know later when J.P. and I ran smack into Luke. Literally. We were turning a corner on our way back to the newspaper office, and Luke was hurrying the other way. We collided.

"Sorry," Luke said, grasping my arm to keep me from falling. "Oh, it's Carlene with the knock-knock jokes."

"Knock knock," I said, picking up the cue.

He grinned. "Who's there?"

"Pecan."

"Pecan who?"

"Pecan somebody your own size."

J.P. giggled. "You're funny, Carlene."

We all laughed. It felt good to laugh. It felt good to put Keith aside for the time being and just be a girl who'd run into a cute guy who was looking at her as if somebody named Angelique didn't even exist.

five

The next couple of days were fun. Angelique must have been out of town, because Luke seemed to be on his own. I didn't ask if the two of them were an item, and he didn't volunteer any information. I knew well enough that Angelique figured they were. That had been evident during the brief moments I'd seen her with him.

To tell the truth, I didn't care. It seemed so natural to be with him, to walk down the street or grab a burger at Ivy's Eats with him, especially to sit at one of the old library tables with him. Fran said they were the same tables that had been in the library when it stood on the original site, which was now under the lake. The tables were stained with ink and pitted with carved initials: "RS was here"; "KC, 1947"; "JW + EK" enclosed in a heart.

Did the JW stand for Jonathan Winward?

I put the thought out of my mind.

We spent a lot of time there at the library. Luke had a part-time summer job with Mariah's newspaper, researching historical stuff and writing a short column that he called "Echoes from the Lake." He said he planned to be a journalist someday and hoped to edit his own newspaper. He was always teasing Mariah about taking her job away from her.

"Fat chance," she'd say, then add something like, "You and your Mongolian hordes don't stand a chance against me and my Amazon maidens."

The second time she said it, I asked Luke what she meant.

He grinned. "Mariah's into past-lives stuff. Some people here in town think she's a little wacko. Don't ask her about it or she'll have you believing you were once Joan of Arc."

So I didn't ask. I was content just to be with Luke. I cleaned the stars and stripes off my fingernails just for him, because the polish was beginning to chip and I didn't want him to think I was a slob or weird for putting it on in the first place. Somehow that seemed significant. I would never have taken off chipped nail polish for any other guy I knew.

We weren't alone when we were together. J.P. was always with us, which was okay with me. Although I had no guilt about trespassing on what Angelique apparently considered her property, I didn't really want to have her ragging on me. Surely she would eventually learn that Luke and I had been hanging out together, but it had to be perfectly innocent, didn't it, with J.P. there?

So my first few days in Lake Isadora passed pleasantly, and I stopped wishing Mom and I could turn right around and go home to Arletta. I was content to sit by Luke's side, searching through dusty books and old newspapers for whatever historical subject he happened to be thinking about at the moment. It seemed so normal. It seemed as if I belonged there beside him.

One day I called him Jonathan.

He gave me a sideways grin. "Old boyfriend?" he asked.

"No," I said, and we dropped the subject.

Mom was the one who was jittery and unsettled. Bud Brady, the "long arm of the law," as Mariah called him, was away somewhere at a convention. The other guy in the two-man police department wasn't helpful. He didn't even take his feet off the desk as he told us Bud was the only person who could approve Mom's handling of the clothing that had been found in the old mine.

"The stuff's locked up in the evidence closet anyways," he said, shifting the toothpick in his mouth from one side to the other. "Bud has the key. He'll be back, come Monday."

So Mom busied herself with getting us set up in the little furnished house Mariah told her about that was for rent. If it hadn't been for Luke, I would have fussed and fretted about settling in that much, a sure indication that we'd be there for a while. But the way things were, I arranged my few possessions happily in the room with the pretty daisy-sprigged wallpaper. It was while I was unpacking that I came upon the binoculars Mom had given me for my birthday.

I took them with me the next day when Luke and J.P. came to pick me up.

"Wow," J.P. said when I showed them to him. Immediately he went outside and aimed the glasses at various landmarks—the lake, the flagpole at the little post office, the unfinished house on top of the hill. "Wow," he repeated. "I can see your grandpa up there, Luke. He's sitting on his front porch, looking out at the lake. He looks so close."

"Well, wave to him," Luke said. "Tell him hi for me."

J.P. waved. "Hi, Jonathan," he said.

Taking the glasses from his eyes, he said, "He can't see me. But he looks close enough for me to touch."

Luke straightened up, tucked his chin down on his

chest, assumed a deep voice, and after a couple of har-
rumphs said, "It's an illusion, created by the prisms
inside the two little telescopes that make up the binoculars, an optical device for use with both eyes, *bi* mean-
ing two."

J.P. sighed. "Sometimes Luke talks like that," he said
to me. "Nobody can understand him. He's smart."
There was a trace of pride in his voice.

"It's my mad scientist act," Luke stage-whispered to
me from the side of his mouth. "Academy Award stuff,
don't you think?"

"Absolutely."

"Really?" J.P. said. "Like on TV?"

"Maybe not." I smiled and rubbed my hand across
J.P.'s buzz cut. But my mind was stuck on the fact that
"the old guy," as J.P. had called him that first day, the
old guy named Jonathan who lived on the hill, was
Luke's grandfather. Did they look alike? Was that why
Luke seemed familiar?

That was dumb. I'd never met Jonathan-on-the-hill.

But when J.P. handed the binocs to me, I raised
them to my eyes and aimed toward Jonathan. The
trouble was, I was looking through them the wrong
way, and Jonathan seemed to retreat from me. It was
almost as if I were gazing at him in the past, far distant
from me but still there. As I watched, he got up from
his chair and walked around the corner of the house.

My heart thudded, and I lowered the binoculars.

"Since we have your nifty glasses," Luke was saying, "let's go down to the lake and look at all the things you can see around the old town, now that the water level is so low. It's gone down so far that you can walk on the foundation of the old schoolhouse and the church."

I flashed for just a microsecond on that old schoolhouse with its three wide cement steps leading up to the front door, its splintery wood floors, its paste-smelling rooms. But then it was gone, and my heart thudded faster.

Actually, I could have been thinking of any of the schools I'd gone to as a child.

"Let's go," I said.

Before we could leave, I had to tell Mom where we were going. She always insisted on knowing where I was at any given time. I understood. She hadn't known Keith had gone to the lake with Dad on the day he disappeared.

"Luke says the water is low enough now that you can see the foundation of the old schoolhouse," I told her.

"Hmm." Mom put an index finger across her lips the way she does when she's thinking. "I guess I should go down to look at it, too. I started school there, you know. So did your dad," she added. "We went there until the town was moved for the lake."

For a moment I thought she was going to say she'd go with us. I didn't want her to do that. In the first place it would look as if she had to go along to protect me like I was a little kid, to make sure that I didn't disappear, too. But more important, it would disturb the balance of the pleasant threesome that Luke, J.P., and I had become in the last couple of days.

"Maybe Mariah and I will go down later," Mom said finally. "Are you taking the binoculars?"

"Yes," I said. "Why?"

"Oh. . . ." Mom seemed to hesitate. "Just in case you see . . . something," she finished.

What "something" did she think I'd see? Maybe Keith still clinging to a tree limb somewhere out in the lake?

The horror of what we might see didn't hit me until Luke, J.P., and I were hiking down the dusty path that led to the lake. Mom was probably thinking that the level of the lake was so low some clues might show up, something that would end the wrenching mystery of what had happened to Keith.

But what if the something was his skeleton?

I wished Bud Brady would return from his lawmen's convention so that we could look at those clothes from the old mine. If they *were* Keith's, then at least I could stop thinking of the hideous things the receding waters might reveal.

If the clothes *were* Keith's, then it was possible that he was still alive.

To put it all out of my mind, I concentrated on J.P.'s cheerful chatter.

"Do you think the fish swam around where the old schoolhouse used to be?" he said. "When the water was deep there, I mean?"

"Sure," Luke said. "You've heard of schools of fish, haven't you?"

J.P.'s eyes widened. "Have I?"

He was wearing his necktie as usual. It hung smoothly across his bare chest from a tidy knot. His aunt probably tied the knot each morning. Or maybe he'd learned to do it himself. It must have once belonged to someone special. His dad, maybe?

Where *was* his dad?

Where was his mother?

What reason could have been big enough for them to leave a neat kid like him behind?

Life was full of mysteries.

Luke was talking about the lake, about the controversies that had held up the construction of the big dam after the government announced that this was the place for it and that the old town would have to be moved. The way he talked, you'd think he'd been there at the time.

I said it. "You make me think you were there on the scene when it all happened."

He grinned. "Maybe I was. Mariah said maybe I was a reporter in a past life and came here to cover the story of the moving of the town."

"That's goofy," I said. "Mariah's goofy if she believes stuff like that."

" 'There are more things in heaven and earth, Horatio, / Than are dreamt of in your philosophy,' " Luke quoted.

"*Hamlet*," I said. "Act one, scene five."

Luke raised his eyebrows. "So you read Shakespeare."

"Not by choice," I said. "My English teacher last year knew *Hamlet* by heart. He always told us that if we were familiar with at least one Shakespeare play, a couple of Gilbert and Sullivan operettas, and knew the first verse of 'The Star-Spangled Banner,' we could get by anywhere."

"Mariah's not goofy," J.P. said.

Oh-oh. I'd forgotten J.P. was a small sponge, soaking up everything he heard.

"Of course not, J.P.," I said. "I was just kidding. Mariah's wonderful."

"She lets me work in her office," J.P. said. "She lets me sort out paper clips and staple stuff together. Sometimes she even pays me a dollar."

Luke winked at me over J.P.'s head. "She lets me work in her office, too. Sometimes she pays me a dollar."

"Maybe she'll let *me* work in her office," I said. "Do you think she would pay me a dollar?"

"Sure, if you work hard," J.P. said seriously. "Maybe she'd let you help Angelique."

Something changed at the mention of her name. It was subtle, but it was there. Did that mean there really was something between her and Luke? I couldn't ask in front of J.P.

I couldn't ask, period.

"Maybe," I said in answer to J.P.'s suggestion. "What does Angelique do?"

"Receptionist and some writing," Luke said briefly.

"Lets me out," I said. "I'm not good at recepting." I looked out across the lake. We were close to it now.

"My brother disappeared on the other side," I said. "Over there where the big trees are."

"You've been here before, then," Luke said.

"No," I said. I hunted through possible explanations of how I knew, but I was saved from saying anything by J.P., who pointed up ahead of us.

"Luke," he said. "There's your grandpa."

At the edge of the receding waters, a man stood looking down toward his feet. He didn't see us, or at least he didn't show that he knew we were there.

As we watched, he bent down to touch something. He seemed to be brushing at it.

As we came closer, we saw that he stood on a cement foundation, about a foot high.

"The old school," Luke said. "He went there when he was a kid. Taught science there after he'd been to college. My grandmother taught there, too. English, I think. I never knew her," he added. "She died before I was born."

The man on the foundation must have heard our voices because now he turned to look at us. He watched silently as we came closer.

"Carlene," Luke said in a low voice. "I love my grandfather. But maybe I should warn you that he might be a little . . ." He seemed to search for words. "A little out of it," he said. His face reddened a little, as if he felt disloyal for saying such a thing about his grandpa. "He had a really bad head injury in an accident on the lake a long time ago."

"What does 'out of it' mean?" J.P. asked.

"Tell you later, pal," Luke said.

His grandfather—Jonathan, I reminded myself— looked nice, neatly dressed in tan slacks and a brown shirt.

He continued to watch us. No, he watched *me*. He seemed puzzled.

Then his face smoothed out and he smiled. A wide, welcoming smile. Eager, almost.

He walked toward us, his eyes on my face. His eyes were tender as he reached out to grasp my hands.

"Elaine," he said in a voice that was feather soft. "I knew you'd come back someday, Elaine."

six

I stepped backward, but not because Jonathan was threatening in any way. In fact, his smile was so gentle, so welcoming, so *sweet*, that I smiled in return.

It was the name that startled me.

"Elaine," Jonathan said. "Want a double- or triple-decker?" We were standing in the door of the ice cream shop, that now familiar shop that smelled of stale sugar and floor polish.

"No," I said. "I'm not Elaine." My throat was tight, and the words came out as a whisper.

Luke touched Jonathan lightly on the arm. "This is Carlene, Grandpa," he said. "*Carlene,*" he said a little louder, as if Jonathan were hard of hearing.

"Who's Elaine?" J.P. asked.

Nobody answered him. Somewhere on the green hillside behind us a cricket sang a short solo. I had the totally irrelevant thought that crickets make their music by rubbing their back legs together. I'd read it somewhere.

Jonathan continued to gaze at me, his eyes luminous. Finally, he nodded. His gentle smile didn't change as he said, "I'm happy to meet you, Carlene. Welcome to Lake Isadora."

"Thank you." I stood there rigidly, staring back at Jonathan. It was with relief that I saw this wasn't the Jonathan I'd remembered in those flashes. That Jonathan had been young, tall and straight, black-haired. This Jonathan was bent just a little. Old. His hair was iron gray.

Oh, but his eyes. I remembered his eyes.

No. No, I didn't. Of course not. They were Luke's eyes, gray-green with flecks of brown in the irises.

I was thinking of Luke's eyes.

I took in a deep, quivery breath. "I'm happy to be here—" I was about to add "Jonathan." But this was an older man. I should show some respect. "I'm happy to be here, Mr. Winward." J.P.'s aunt had said that was Jonathan's last name.

He nodded and made a sweeping gesture toward the lake with one arm. "Interesting time to come here. You can see the old foundations. The schoolhouse and the church and the old hotel. Some of the houses."

I could feel him watching me closely, as if to note my reaction to what he'd said.

I was careful not to show *any* reaction. What was he looking for anyway? "That's what Luke said." I kept my voice interested but calm. "Is that where the school-house was?" I pointed, knowing well enough that's where it had been. I knew where the big double front door used to be, and that the first room on the left had been Miss Oliverson's.

Ignoring the memories that suddenly flooded the spaces of my brain, I walked toward the foundations. Dead weeds rattled as I walked through them, their pungent smell bringing back even more memories.

Jonathan walked beside me, with Luke and J.P. following. "Luke said it was a school for fishes when the water was deep," J.P. said.

Jonathan laughed. "Probably was. Do you think they had classes in water polo?"

J.P. giggled.

Luke seemed to relax, and I wondered if it was because Jonathan (try as I might, I couldn't think of him as Mr. Winward) was acting totally normal now. He was nice. I liked him, and if he hadn't called me Elaine when he first saw me I would never have known there was anything different about him.

So why *had* he called me Elaine?

Who was she? I wasn't sure I wanted to know.

"The little church was over there." Jonathan pointed to a spot behind the schoolhouse. "That's where . . ."

He paused, looking at me, then went on. "That's where I was married. And down that way was the general store and the ice cream parlor."

Where the lady who ran the shop sometimes added another scoop for no better excuse than that the sun was bright or the wind was blowing from the west. And farther down along the street was an old blacksmith shop with a huge anvil and a glowing forge and bellows.

Was the forge still there?

What did I know about forges?

Feeling as if I were suffocating, I walked swiftly away from the schoolhouse foundation, down along the old street now lined by dead willows. I'd heard once that hair still grows after a person is dead. Was that the way it had been with the willows? Had they grown along the old dead streets after the town had drowned? My brother Keith could have gotten tangled in them that day eighteen years ago. Maybe they had reached out languid limbs to hold him there, claiming him, keeping him under the water to play on the streets where live children had once played. Was I going to come upon something of him there? Was that why I kept recalling things I couldn't possibly know anything about?

"Carlene."

I almost screamed at the sound of my name, but then I realized it was just J.P. He'd come up behind me and was holding my binoculars out toward me.

"Want to look through these?" he said.

"Sure." I took them, holding them up to my eyes. Wasn't that why Mom had given them to me, so I could look for Keith?

The dry willows clacked in the faint breeze as I turned slowly in a full circle, scanning the still water of what was left of the lake, the mountains behind, the new town in the distance, the cabin that Mom had said belonged to someone named Perla, and the tables and benches of the recreation area up by the trees that had marked the shoreline before the drought.

Turning the glasses back toward the old schoolhouse foundation, I saw Jonathan and Luke still standing there. They were talking together. About me?

No, why should they? They were probably discussing an article Luke was writing, or maybe just deciding what groceries Jonathan needed to buy before he returned to his unfinished house on the hill. *From which you could see the entire lake if you looked to the south. To the north there were the mounds of dirt from the old mine still visible in the distance.*

I brought my thoughts back to what I was seeing now. *Right now.* What I saw was a little white convertible stopping on the highway above where the schoolhouse was. The driver was a girl. Without getting out, she raised up and waved to Luke and Jonathan, then gestured for them to come closer.

"That's Angelique's car," J.P. said, squinting in the sunlight.

So Angelique was home from wherever she'd been. And she was motioning for Luke, not Luke *and* Jonathan, to come to her.

I saw Luke start climbing the rocky hill up toward the car. Feeling guilty about watching, I backed up until I was almost hidden by the willows.

"She likes Luke," J.P. said.

Something in his tone told me that he didn't fully approve. Of what? Of Angelique? Or of Angelique liking Luke?

When Luke reached the car, Angelique leaned out over the door to kiss him. He didn't appear to resist.

I lowered the glasses. Oh well. It had been nice while it lasted. Maybe Mom and I would be leaving soon anyway. Tomorrow Bud Brady would be back, then Mom could see the clothing that had been found in the old mine. It wouldn't be Keith's. And I had seen no clue of him there at the lake. After all this time it was ludicrous to think there might be anything.

So we would go back to Arletta, and Mom would file Keith away in that place where you keep memories of the dead.

And I would file Luke away in the place where you keep memories of lost loves.

Oh, for crying out loud, he was no lost love. He was just a nice friend I'd met here in this place where I didn't want to be.

"Let's go back to Jonathan." I held out a hand to J.P.

He reached for it, then stopped. "Do you mind touching my wart?" he asked.

"No," I said. "I had warts when I was your age."

"Really?" Carefully he placed his hand in mine. I could feel the rough bump on his thumb.

"Really," I said. "Three of them. One on my left hand and two on my right."

He turned his eyes up to me. "How'd you get rid of them?"

I shrugged. "They just went away as I got older."

"Good," J.P. said. "Mariah said somebody in a book thought he could get rid of warts by taking a dead cat to a graveyard at midnight and heaving it after a bad guy."

"I think she meant *Tom Sawyer*," I said. "I read that book, too. But you don't have to heave a dead cat to get rid of the warts."

J.P. took in a deep breath and let it out in a sigh of relief. "I'd rather keep them than do that." He gave a happy skip.

I thought about how much J.P.'s runaway mother was missing by not being part of his life.

My own mother had missed being part of Keith's life when he was that age. I hadn't thought about that before.

When we were almost back to the schoolhouse foundation, I looked up again to the highway. I could see well enough now without the binocs. Well enough to know that Angelique was not happy about something.

She was talking, making little jerks of her head for emphasis.

Luke pointed back toward the lake. Toward Jonathan and J.P. Toward me.

Angelique flounced down in the seat and started the car, leaving in a spurt of rocks from the tires.

Luke watched her go, then turned to come down the hill.

It was on the way back to town that I finally got the courage to ask the question I'd been avoiding. Jonathan had gone his own way, and Luke and J.P. and I were heading back to the newspaper office where Luke was supposed to finish an article he'd been writing.

I cleared my throat before speaking. "Who is Elaine?" I asked.

"She was my grandmother," Luke said. "She died a long time ago. Drowned in the lake."

"When?" I forced myself to ask.

"Eighteen years ago," Luke said. "She died trying to save a little boy from drowning."

For about three more steps there was silence. Then Luke stopped, staring at me. It was like in cartoons when a light goes on above somebody's head. "She died trying to save your brother," he said slowly. "I've known the story of her drowning all of my life, but I didn't connect it to Keith until right now."

J.P. looked puzzled as he glanced at me. "But why did Jonathan call *you* Elaine?"

I knew the answer now. But I wasn't going to say it. I was going to ignore the fact that I knew, because I couldn't deny it. Not when the memories kept filling my mind.

I needed to talk to Mariah, who believed she had lived before.

seven

I didn't get to talk to Mariah right away. When Luke, J.P., and I got back to the newspaper office, Mom was there, all excited.

"Bud Brady called," she told me. "He's back in town. He'll show us the clothing that was found in the old mine as soon as we can get to the police station."

She seemed breathless, and her cheeks were red as if she'd been running.

Mariah put a hand on her arm. "Jen," she began.

Mom nodded. "I know, I know. I shouldn't get my hopes up too much. But—" She paused and I saw tears sparkle in her eyes.

Both Mariah and I stepped forward to hug her. J.P., who didn't really know what was going on, pushed in, too, and wrapped his arms around Mom's waist.

She looked down at his wheat-colored buzz cut, and

that undid her more than anything else. She hadn't really cried since we'd arrived in Lake Isadora, but now she hugged J.P. and wept in great, wrenching sobs.

"It's okay," he said, reaching up to pat her back. "It's okay."

I wondered who patted *his* back when he was unhappy and told him "It's okay." Fran, most likely, or maybe Mariah, since I doubted if his mother had been around long enough to take care of his kid hurts.

Luke stood to one side, watching. Finally he said, "Hey, J.P. buddy, how about helping me write my story while the others go check things out?"

J.P. looked up at Mom. "Can't I go with you?"

Pulling a tissue from a pocket of her skirt, she wiped her face. "Maybe it would be better if you stay here with Luke. We'll tell you everything that happens as soon as we get back."

"Is this about Keith?" J.P. asked.

"Maybe," Mom said.

"If you find him," J.P. said, "tell him I'll be his friend. I'll show him stuff about school and all. He looks nice."

Mom glanced at me, puzzlement in her eyes.

"We saw his picture on the computer at the library," I explained. "J.P.'s aunt Fran found it."

Mom didn't bother to explain to J.P. that the picture he'd seen was more than eighteen years old and that

Keith would be in his twenties now. "He'd like you to be his friend, J.P.," she said. "He'd like that a lot."

Mom, Mariah, and I walked together to the little police station. I noticed Mom had dressed up for the occasion in her favorite red-flowered skirt and a red blouse. Was red for courage? Or maybe it had been Keith's favorite color.

As that thought crossed my mind, I flashed again on a small boy in a red shirt. *Plaid, it was, but mostly red. Striped overalls. A blue cap, with a bill. He was holding on to someone's hand. His face was tilted up, and he seemed to be saying something. I saw the curve of his cheek, round and rosy as a peach.* Before the vision faded, I looked quickly at the person whose hand he held. A man. Was it Dad? A much younger Dad than the one I knew?

My heart thudded. Where had the vision, or apparition, or whatever it was, come from? Had it been there in my memory from another time, another life?

Or was there a perfectly logical explanation? I was sure I'd seen that picture in Grandma's photo album. Or *almost* sure.

I wished I'd stayed back at the newspaper office with Luke and J.P.

I wished I'd had a chance to talk to Mariah before we started for the police station.

But we were there now, and there didn't seem to be any way I could suddenly desert Mom.

The deputy we'd seen before was sitting in the little outer room, his feet on the desk as if he hadn't moved at all since we'd been there last. His hair appeared to have been in a whirlwind, and there was a short stand of stubble on his cheeks.

"Hi, Arnie," Mariah said. "We've come to see Bud."

"Yeah," Arnie said. "He said you were coming. Go on in." Without removing his feet from the desk, he flipped a thumb toward a closed door that had the words "Barton Brady, Chief" painted on it in block lettering.

If the frowsy deputy was the only officer he was chief over, I wasn't too impressed by Barton Brady and the Lake Isadora Police Department.

Oh, Mom, I pleaded silently, *let's forget this and go back home.* I couldn't imagine that these guys could follow a clue if it marched right up and smacked them in the face.

Mariah opened the door and walked in, motioning for Mom and me to follow.

"Hello, Bud," she said. "Brought somebody you haven't seen for half a lifetime."

Bud Brady was standing by a filing cabinet, poking through an open drawer. He was tall and lanky and wore a crisp, well-fitting tan uniform. He had dark, neatly combed hair, and when he turned around I looked into the most piercing blue eyes I'd ever seen.

I revised my opinion of the Lake Isadora Police Department.

"Jen!" he exclaimed as he walked over to Mom and wrapped his long arms around her. "I haven't seen you since—"

He stopped, then took a step backward and looked at her.

"Since Keith disappeared," Mom finished for him. "It's okay, Bud. It happened." She turned to me. "This is my daughter, Carlene."

Bud turned those blue eyes to me. "You look just like your mother did back in high school." He put out a hand. I took it and was reassured by his warm, friendly grip. Maybe we *would* be able to find out something about Keith, with his help. He seemed totally capable and efficient.

But if he was so capable, why hadn't he found out something about Keith a long time ago?

Why hadn't he figured out himself that the clothes found in the mine might be Keith's?

As if he read my mind, he answered that question.

"I should have thought about contacting you, Jen," he said, "when we first found those clothes. But Keith disappeared so long ago that I guess we've just closed the books on him. Didn't occur to me to connect those clothes with your boy until Mariah told me you were coming here."

As he spoke, he opened a desk drawer and took out a key. Striding over to a door at the back of the room, he inserted the key into the lock and opened it.

Things were moving too fast. *Stop,* I wanted to say. *Let me catch my breath before I see those clothes.* What if he brought out a red plaid shirt and striped overalls?

I sat down on a straight chair beside Bud's desk. Taking deep breaths, I watched as he took a black plastic bag from the closet.

"Sit down, Jen," he said to Mom, who hovered close to him. "I don't know whether these things have anything to do with Keith or not, but maybe you'd better be sitting." His voice was warm and full of sympathy.

Mom sat on the brown leather sofa, which stretched the length of one wall of the small room. Mariah sat down beside her.

"Here they are," Bud said, pulling some things from the plastic bag and spreading them out on the low table in front of the sofa. "They're dirty from having been in that mine for so long, but you might be able to recognize them if . . . you know."

I closed my eyes, my heart thudding again. If, when I opened them, I saw the red plaid shirt I was sure I'd choke.

I heard Mom gasp.

Dragging my eyes open, I saw a small pair of sage-green shorts and a faded little T-shirt that looked as if it had once had green stripes.

My stomach lurched, and I felt as if I were in a pitching boat. *Someone was yelling. Several people, actually. One of them was me.*

Beside me, somebody swung a pair of oars, trying to maneuver closer to another boat.

Jonathan. Arms bare, muscles bulging, he pulled at the oars.

The wind howled. We were both drenched, but whether from rain or from the choppy water of the lake, I didn't know.

In the other boat were two people, someone in a yellow slicker and hat and a small boy who clung to the sides and looked across the water at me.

I reached out as the two boats came close together. "Grab my hands," I yelled to the boy, who I could now see was Keith Carter.

"No!" he screamed. "I want my daddy."

The boats separated. The one with Keith in it was almost totally swamped now.

Jonathan wrestled with the oars. "Try again, Elaine," he shouted at me.

Again I reached out toward Keith. "Come to me," I said, as gently as I could. "Then we'll get your daddy."

This time Keith stood up. He wore sage-green shorts and a green-striped T-shirt.

"Carlene," I heard Mom saying. She sounded far away. "Carlene, you look as if you're going to faint."

"I am," I said.

But I didn't. Instead I clung to the desk beside my chair, the only stable thing in the drenched, pitching world I was still part of.

"Where's my daddy?" Keith screamed. "He's . . ." The wind carried away the rest of what he said.

Leaning as far out of the boat as I could, I reached for the little boy. Our hands touched.

"Carlene!"

Someone was shaking me.

The wind ceased abruptly, and I was back in Bud Brady's office. Mariah stood over me.

"Sorry," she said. "But I had to bring you back from wherever you were."

"Carlene," Mom said, "are you all right?"

She was still on the sofa, so pale that I knew she didn't have the strength to move from it. She'd picked up the clothes and was clutching them tightly.

"Carlene," she said again. "What's the matter?"

"Those clothes," I whispered. "Keith was wearing them on the day he disappeared."

eight

Nobody said anything. The silence seemed to suck the air out of the room so that I could scarcely breathe.

"Those are Keith's clothes," I said, as if they hadn't heard me the first time.

Mom drew a deep, shuddering breath. "Yes, they are." All the worry lines smoothed out so that her face looked young and radiant. "I've known all along that he's alive."

I couldn't tell her any different. Certainly he'd been alive in my vision, as far as it went.

But then so had Elaine.

What had happened after that? Had Elaine been able to pull Keith into the boat with her and Jonathan? I remembered the touch of his small hand. I remembered trying to look into the face of the other person in that boat.

It should have been my father, shouldn't it? Who else would Keith be with in a boat?

But I couldn't tell who it was, bundled as he was in the yellow slicker and hat. Had Dad brought the rain gear with him from home? But he would never have taken Keith out on the lake if he had known ahead of time that there would be a bad storm. So it couldn't be my dad.

Mom's face was unreal. It seemed to be lit up from somewhere deep inside. Her eyes glowed.

It spooked me a little when she turned those glowing eyes toward me. "How did *you* know, Carlene? How did you know these are Keith's clothes?"

I didn't know how I knew. What was it that had gone on inside my brain, showing me a scene from that long-ago day as clearly as if it were a video?

"I just know," I whispered lamely.

Mariah shot me a quizzical glance. I looked back at her. *Not yet,* I tried to tell her without words. *We'll talk about it later.*

Mom accepted what I said, without question. "He's alive," she murmured.

There was something wrong with my ears. Her soft words sounded to me as if she'd spoken them into an echo chamber. Maybe I was going to pass out after all.

I became aware that Bud was speaking. Something

about not getting our hopes up yet. It was too soon, he said. After all, we didn't *know* Keith was alive.

Mom shook her head. "We'll find him. He's *some-where.*"

"It's been eighteen years, Jen," Bud said. "Where will we start looking?"

She smiled at him. A bright, blazing smile, as if that light inside had gone up a few hundred watts. "Any-where," she said. "Everywhere. He's alive. He has to be *somewhere.*"

Bud pulled up a chair and sat down facing her. "We'll do all we can. But if he's alive, he's probably had a different name all these years. I mean, if somebody took him they'd change his name. He probably doesn't even remember where he came from. Besides, just because we found the clothes doesn't mean—"

He didn't finish his sentence. We all knew what he meant. Finding Keith's clothes didn't prove a thing.

Mom's smile didn't dim. She hugged those clothes to her chest and said, "We found one clue. We'll find others."

I wondered what she'd say if I tried to tell her about the visions of Keith I'd seen. I was thinking of them as visions now, because I wasn't sure they really were memories. At least not until I'd had a chance to talk to Mariah.

• • •

I've heard people say that someone walked on air, but I thought it was just a figure of speech until I saw how Mom practically floated back to the newspaper office. I could see she wasn't aware of where she was or whom she was walking with. She was somewhere else.

Perhaps her unfailing faith that Keith was alive had caused those visions to come to me. It wasn't any harder to believe than that I had once been Elaine. Elaine, who apparently knew what had happened to Keith. Who took this knowledge with her to her watery grave.

I turned off those thoughts. They made me dizzy and nauseated.

Neither J.P. nor Luke was at the newspaper office when we got there. In fact, the whole place was quiet and deserted. Not even any noise from the back room where the presses were.

Mom started telling Mariah right off that she should write an article about the clothes to be in the next issue, which was due out in two days. It was a weekly newspaper, distributed each Thursday.

"We'll call the TV stations over in Bakersfield," Mom said, "and contact some of the big city newspapers, like the *Los Angeles Times*. We've got to get the word out. Someone will remember a little blond boy who must have cried for his mother. Someone will remember, even after all these years."

Mariah led her over to the desk and sat her down on a swivel chair. "Jen," she said. "Listen to me. Let Bud handle this. Let him call the shots. Let the police do their work."

Mom jumped to her feet and jittered over to the window. "But we can help. Somebody, somewhere, will have a memory of that day. How will we ever find them if we don't tell people?"

Mariah led her back to the chair and pushed her down onto it again. "Let's say that somebody took him that day," she said.

"Somebody did," I said. "Somebody had him in a boat."

Mariah's head snapped in my direction, but Mom didn't even seem to have heard. She was in her own world.

"Let's say," Mariah went on as if I hadn't said anything, "that this person who took him has lived all these years without anybody finding out, so he feels perfectly safe by now. If he finds out we're looking for him, won't he make absolutely sure we don't find anything? Didn't you listen to what Bud said?"

Mom nodded, but I didn't remember what Bud had said. I'd been so swallowed up by my efforts to separate myself from Elaine that I hadn't heard much of anything for a while.

"But we have to do *something*, Mariah," Mom said.

Her face still had that glow from within. "Am I supposed to just sit around and twiddle my thumbs now that I know for sure Keith is alive?"

"No." Mariah picked up a pad and pencil. "Here's what you can do. First, call your mother and tell her about the clothes." She scribbled on the pad as she spoke. "Second, call Carl and tell him."

"I don't even know how to get in touch with him," Mom said. "He hasn't contacted us for years. He's out of our lives."

"Okay," Mariah said. She crossed out what she'd just written. "Third, or second as the case may be, go back to your house and lie down. This has been a devastating day. Maybe we should call Orvid Knight and have him give you a sedative."

Orvid Knight was apparently a doctor. Maybe he could turn off the light inside Mom that made her look almost transparent. I didn't like her looking that way.

Why not? Was I jealous that the idea of Keith being alive could make her light up?

No, no, it wasn't anything like that. It was just because the light seemed unnatural. Unhealthy. Unwholesome, almost.

There was a small ripping sound as Mariah tore the top sheet off the pad she'd been writing on. Handing it to Mom, she said, "Here. Use the telephone right there on the desk."

Mom looked dazed, but she took the paper.

"Carlene and I will leave you alone for a few minutes," Mariah said. "Is that okay?"

Mom twirled around on the swivel chair. "Okeydokey," she said.

I'd never heard her say "okeydokey" before.

She was acting so strange that I really didn't want to leave her alone. But Mariah took my hand and pulled me through the opening in the counter, then down the hallway to a room filled with computers and printers.

"Okay, Carlene," she said, motioning for me to sit. "Tell me."

I knew what she meant. So I told her everything. Right from the day we'd arrived and I'd "remembered" Jonathan and the ice cream parlor. And the school. Even the familiar smells, and the things I'd touched. I told her how I'd tasted the apples and ice cream. And there were all the other things I couldn't possibly remember since they hadn't happened to *me*. Everything, right up through the vision of me and Jonathan in the boat, trying to save Keith.

She didn't say anything when I finished.

"Mariah," I said. "What's going on?"

"Don't you know?" she asked softly.

"I was Elaine." I stopped to take a deep breath. "I lived another life before this one."

She gazed steadily at me.

"But that's not possible," I said.

"Why not?"

"Things like that don't happen."

"Why not?" she asked again.

"It would mean that—" I paused, searching for some kind of logic in what I was going to say. "It would mean that Elaine was *recycled* after she died."

Mariah laughed. "Good way of putting it," she said. "Reincarnated might be a better way to phrase it. Many people believe that after we die we are born again to live another life. They believe we experience a reembodiment."

"And you're one of those people who believe?"

Mariah nodded.

I shook my head in disbelief. "How can that work?"

"I don't know," Mariah said. "How can jet engines work? Or modems? Or birth and death?"

I didn't know what to say.

Mariah gave a little laugh. "Some people around here think I'm a crackpot. But there are some things that can't be explained by conventional thought."

I still didn't say anything.

"Okay," Mariah said. "You believe that souls live on after death, don't you?"

"Yes, I do," I said.

"If there's something important enough that a soul who has died needs to communicate it, why is it so hard to believe the soul might be given another chance?"

I heard some kind of machinery start up in the back room. Someone had apparently come back to the office.

I shook my head. "It's too weird."

Mariah gazed out the window beyond the computers and printers. "You still read Shakespeare in school, right?"

What did that have to do with anything? "Yes," I said. "We read *Hamlet* last year. Mr. Taylor made us practically memorize it."

"Remember when Hamlet is telling Horatio about the ghost, and Horatio can't accept the strangeness of it?"

Luke and I had just been through this a few days before. "'There are more things in heaven and earth, Horatio, / Than are dreamt of in your philosophy.'" I gave Mariah a small grin. "Mr. Taylor told us that when we could apply what we were reading to real life, we'd begin to understand what it is to be educated."

Mariah smiled.

I took a deep breath. "So do you really think I was Elaine?"

"What do you think?" she asked.

"But why would she come back as me? As Keith's sister?"

She smiled, as if she thought I was finally getting

it. "Think about it," she said. "She apparently saw something that's vitally important to him. The two of you are connected by that event. She probably came back as Keith's sister to—" She paused, looking at me expectantly.

"To let us know what happened to my brother," I finished for her.

nine

Mariah's smile was almost as bright as Mom's had been. "Yes!" she said. "Think what this means, Carlene."

I felt shaky, as if I'd had the flu for a couple of weeks. "How can it mean anything? It's been eighteen years. How can we find him now?" I seemed to be repeating Bud Brady's words. So I'd experienced the memories of a dead woman, and I'd seen Keith in a boat with someone on a stormy lake. Where did we go from there?

"Elaine would have known my dad, wouldn't she?" I said. "She would have recognized him if he was in the boat with Keith, wouldn't she?"

Mariah didn't ask where that question came from. "Your father had been a student of Elaine's at the high school. We were all in her English classes. Yes, she would have recognized him." Now she looked quizzically at me.

"I didn't know the man in the boat," I said. "Which

means Elaine didn't know him. Actually, according to what I saw, she couldn't see his face. It couldn't have been my dad, because he was trapped under his boat. We know that now. Right?"

"Right," Mariah said. "He didn't see anything that happened."

I nodded. "Okay, this other guy—let's say he did take Keith that day—how would we start looking for him?"

Mariah reached out to lay a hand over one of mine. "There may be more memories, Carlene. We'll have to see if we can get to them."

I shrank back a little, not wanting to think about going back to that pitching boat. "But I never know when they're going to come," I said. "I don't know how to get to them."

"We'll go after them, Carlene." Mariah's bright smile refused to fade. "They must be there, somewhere in your brain. We'll find them."

I visualized Mariah probing my brain with something like a nutpick. She'd drill a hole in my skull and go inside to locate those memories, all neatly packaged like a videotape that she'd shove into a VCR and—lo!— there would be the information we needed.

I was really going wacko. I stood up. "Not today," I said, not even asking how Mariah planned to find the memories. I didn't want to know. "I'm going to go see how Mom is."

Mariah didn't object. Standing up, she said, "Write everything down, Carlene. All that you remember about being in the boat."

"*You* write it down," I said. "I've told you everything. Jonathan and I were in one boat, and we were trying to reach Keith in the other boat with this guy whose face I couldn't see." I started for the outer office, then stopped short. "Jonathan!" I said.

"What about him?" Mariah said.

I turned to face her. "He was there! Doesn't he remember all this? Can't he tell you as much as I can?"

"He was hurt," Mariah said. "A head injury. If he saw something significant, he doesn't remember it. Would you like to talk to him, Carlene?"

I slumped. "No," I said. "But maybe I should. He called me Elaine, you know."

Mariah nodded. "I know. You told me."

Suddenly it seemed urgent that I talk to him. "Can we go see Jonathan now?" I asked.

"I'll call and see if he's home."

"Are we going to tell him about my memories?"

Mariah paused, considering it. "Not right away. Let's just talk to him."

I looked toward the outer office. "What about Mom? Am I going to tell her the whole story right now?" I remembered how she'd looked on the way back to the newspaper office. As if she were in another world, one filled with hope and the possibility that she and Keith would be reunited. One in which I scarcely existed. I wasn't sure there would be a place for me in her life if we *did* find Keith. Maybe I'd go back to being Elaine, after my purpose for living again was over. Poor drowned Elaine. I didn't know how these things worked. Maybe Carlene would be wiped out.

Mariah was standing silently beside me. She seemed to be thinking. "No," she said. "We won't tell your mother about this yet. She's had enough for today. The high she's on right now will carry her through for a while. We'll tell her when the time is right."

By that time I might have had more visions. Or Jonathan could have remembered something. Maybe we'd have something to go on.

Mariah, Mom, and I walked up the hill to Jonathan's "skeleton" house, as J.P. had called it. Mariah said it would be good for us to walk, to drain off some of the nervous energy.

I'd wanted Mom to go back to our little rented house and rest as Mariah had suggested, but she was too excited to settle down. She'd talked to Grandma, who was cautious about reviving hope, Mom said. She had no idea where to call Dad.

I suspected she didn't want to share these coming days with Dad anyway. He'd refused to believe there was any possibility that Keith was alive and had left us because Mom wouldn't give up hope.

So now we were trudging up the steep hill, and I was searching around in my memories for other instances when I'd climbed that same hill, as Elaine.

I didn't find any.

I'd brought my binoculars with me, and we stopped now and then to focus them on the valley. The lake appeared withdrawn, receding from the shoreline it had made over the years. It seemed to seclude itself behind small hills, only to glitter unexpectedly from hidden valleys. There were thunderclouds to the north, and the lake looked dark and secretive in the murky light. I had the thought that I was looking at the place where Elaine had died. Where *I* had died.

I shut out the thought, put my binoculars back in their case, and plodded on toward Jonathan's house.

He was waiting for us on his front porch, in the same rocker he'd sat in on the day J.P. first pointed him out to me. There was another rocker beside him. Elaine's maybe? Would it still be there, after all the years that had passed?

But wouldn't I have some twinge of memory if Elaine had once sat there?

Jonathan rose as we came up the porch steps. "Quite a climb, isn't it? I could have driven down to pick you up, you know."

"It's good for us," Mariah puffed. "Gets the printer's ink out of our lungs and puts roses in Carlene's cheeks." She didn't mention what it did for Mom. Her cheeks had already been flushed and her eyes unnaturally bright even before we'd started up the hill.

Jonathan smiled at me, and there was none of the soft recognition that had been in his eyes that first time he saw me. "This old house could use a few roses. Would you like to come inside?" He motioned a hand toward the door.

"Why don't we sit out here?" I said. "I like the view."

I wasn't up to looking inside the house yet. Elaine's house, unfinished since her death, Luke had told me. I didn't know what surprises might lurk in its corners, waiting to draw me into the strange world of past lives.

Jonathan pulled up chairs for Mariah and himself, indicating that Mom and I should sit in the rockers. He chatted briefly with Mom, something about not having seen her for a long time and what a good student she'd been when he was her science teacher. Then he asked, "Like some root beer, anybody? It's homemade."

Made from extract, with yeast and sugar and water added. Left in a warm place for a couple of days before being put on ice.

Another of Elaine's memories.

"Later," Mariah said. "Have you heard, Jonathan,

that those clothes in the old mine did belong to Keith Carter?"

Jonathan's eyebrows went up. He gazed at Mom, whose smile was brighter than the afternoon sun. "You don't say so! Could mean that he's alive, then." He turned his eyes back to Mariah. "Could be somebody took him to the old mine to change to a dry outfit. Or to disguise the way he looked."

"Exactly." Mariah looked at me. "We thought we'd find out what you remember about the day he disappeared," she said to Jonathan. "We're looking for some kind of clue that will tell us where to go from here."

"Can't be much help," Jonathan said. "Elaine and I were trying to get close enough to the boat Keith was in to reach out and get him. The water was really rough and kept pulling the other boat away from us."

"Could you see who the other person was?" I asked.

"I don't think so." Jonathan frowned. "I can't say for sure because I must have slipped and cracked my head on the side of the boat or something. Don't remember anything after that until I woke up in the hospital. That's when they told me Elaine—" He stopped.

There was silence for a few seconds.

"That's about it," Jonathan said. "Elaine was gone. Keith was gone. Elaine's body eventually washed up on those rocks by Perla's cabin a couple of days later.

Never any sign of Keith." He rubbed a hand across his eyes. "Could be good news that you found his clothes."

We heard voices then, from the other side of the house.

Jonathan stood up. "Sounds like Luke. Said he was going to come up this afternoon. Must be somebody with him."

The somebody was J.P. He was dressed as usual in khaki shorts and his necktie.

"Hi, Carlene," he said when he saw me. "We wondered where you'd gone."

We? Did that mean Luke had wondered, too? Had he missed me? Had he come looking for me?

Don't be silly, I told myself. Jonathan said Luke planned to come up this afternoon.

He was looking at me as if he was glad I was there. "Hi, Carlene," he said, echoing J.P.

I smiled at him. "Hi, yourself." To J.P. I said, "Knock knock."

His eyes lit up. "Who's there?"

"Plato."

"Plato who?"

"Plato spaghetti and meatballs, please," I said.

J.P. giggled. "Carlene knows lots of knock-knocks," he told Jonathan. "She's funny."

Jonathan gave me a curious look. "Elaine knew lots of knock-knocks, too," he said softly.

I didn't have to respond to that because J.P. wiped his forehead with a grimy hand and said, "I'm hot from climbing up that hill. You got any root beer?"

"Sure do," Jonathan said. "Why don't you and Carlene and Luke go get us each a glassful?"

"Okay." J.P. put out a hand toward me. It was the warty one, and he quickly changed to the other hand. "Come on, Carlene."

Putting my binoculars on the seat of the rocker, I took his hand, extending my other hand to Luke. "Come on, Luke." His hand was big and warm. A nice hand. I realized it was the first time I'd touched him.

I wondered where Angelique was.

"I like Jonathan's root beer better than anything," J.P. said. "Better than ice cream. Better than peanut butter."

I remembered another little boy coming into my kitchen, saying he liked root beer best of all.

"Better than cake, Keith?" I said. "Better than chocolate chip cookies with oatmeal and coconut?"

"Better than anything, Elaine," Keith said. He went to the three-sided cupboard in the corner and took out three plastic mugs shaped like cowboy boots. After setting them on the counter, he opened the refrigerator and took out a bottle of the homemade root beer I'd made the week before.

90

My heart thudded. I seemed caught in some kind of time warp as I watched J.P. go to the same cupboard and take out three plastic mugs. Three mugs shaped like cowboy boots.

There was no longer any question in my mind that I had once been Elaine.

ten

Sometimes you have to set aside everything you believe in order to accept a new fact. Since I now knew that I was once Elaine, I had to set aside all my previous beliefs about life (one per person) and death (die, go to heaven). I had to accept the fact that I'd lived another life before this present one. So did that make me a used soul? Like a used car that has had a previous existence before you get it?

But it was I, not Elaine, who decided to tell everybody there at Jonathan's house about what I now knew to be true.

So after J.P. and I served glasses of icy cold homemade root beer to everyone, I made an announcement. But not before I sent J.P. back into the house to watch TV for a little while.

"I'll watch *Lion King*," he said. "Jonathan keeps the video here for me. I've watched it seventeen times."

"Maybe you'd like to watch something else then," I said.

J.P. shook his head. He took a sip of his root beer, then looked up through his lashes. "No," he said, a little shyly. "If I watch it enough, maybe sometime the King won't die."

I didn't tell him that it was in the script for the Lion King to die. That that's the way it was written and that it wasn't going to change no matter how often he watched it. It had to be that way to teach that goodness conquers and that what the King had taught his son would live on.

So was it written in my script that I had to live again as Keith's sister so we could all learn something? Learn what? That families are forever, like Grandma's wall hanging said? But wasn't there a twist in that somewhere? I mean, if families are forever, which family did I belong to? Was I Elaine, or was I Carlene? Did I have *two* forever families? Were there more lives, more families, I didn't know about?

"I have something to say," I announced to Mom, Jonathan, Luke, and Mariah out on the porch as soon as J.P. was settled inside in front of the TV.

I immediately regretted it. I should have consulted Mariah first. I should have considered what effect it would have on Jonathan. And what would it do to Mom?

Mariah must have guessed what I was going to do, because she gave me an encouraging smile. Maybe she just trusted me to do the right thing, which was a laugh because I was in totally foreign territory.

But now I'd started, I had to go on. I began as I'd done with Mariah, telling about the first strange experience on the day we'd arrived in Lake Isadora. I went on to tell everything that had happened, right up to the vision, or whatever it was, concerning Keith and the root beer.

I tried not to look at Mom as I spoke. She still had the unnatural glow that had been with her ever since we'd seen Keith's clothes at Bud Brady's office. She seemed almost like a stranger, someone I didn't know.

I sensed she was watching me closely as I told my story. When I finished, she rose slowly and came over to hug me gently. "Oh, Carlene," she said. "I *knew* there was some reason you were born. You're going to bring Keith back to me." Pulling her chair over beside mine, she sat down, hanging on to my hand as if that would bring her closer to Keith.

I'm sure she didn't realize the incredible cruelty of what she'd said. To think that I'd been born just to bring back my lost brother was devastating. Was I expendable? My earlier questions came back to me. Would my identity as Carlene end as soon as I fulfilled the mission of restoring my brother to his family? Would I then retire into Elaine's grave?

Thinking of Elaine prompted me to look at Jonathan. He sat gazing at me, his eyes soft and warm, the way they'd been that first day he'd seen me. The day he'd called me Elaine.

Luke was looking back and forth from me to Jonathan. Suddenly he stood up. "Isn't somebody going to say something?" he said. "About how ridiculous this is? I mean, am I supposed to believe that Carlene was once my grandmother? Am I supposed to call her Grandma now? This is all so lame. It's totally senseless." He took a couple of steps toward the edge of the porch as if he were going to run away.

Mariah stood up to stop him. "Wait," she said. "Listen to me. Something wonderful has happened here. Let's think it through."

She gently pushed Luke back onto his chair but remained standing herself. "Let me say something first." She turned to Mom. "Let's get this straight, Jen. Carlene was born to live her own life. Not just to bring Keith back. That would be a bonus, if it really does come to pass."

Mom didn't say anything, but her hopefulness almost outshone the sun.

"And, Luke." Mariah turned to him. "There really

is sense to all of this. Carlene isn't your grandmother. She's Carlene. She's not related to you in any way. It's just that apparently she once lived as Elaine, whose life was cut short by an accident. During that accident she saw something that just might be the answer to what happened to Keith. Perhaps we are *meant* to find out where he is. It makes a lot of sense that Elaine would be reembodied as someone who can help him. Help *us*."

So wasn't she saying just about the same thing as Mom said, only not in such a cruel way? My life at this moment seemed to be following some cosmic script. I was supposed to give some information about Keith. But what came next? What were my lines?

Jonathan spoke for the first time. "Bless you, Carlene," he whispered.

Before we could say anything more, J.P. came back to the porch. He was crying, wiping his eyes with his necktie. "The Lion King died again," he said.

We'd all had enough for one day. Mom asked Mariah if Perla Goudy still lived in town. Mariah said she didn't, but that she turned up at her cabin on the lakeshore now and then, just for a few days. I asked Mom who this Perla was, remembering that we'd looked at her cabin through my binoculars the first day we arrived. Jonathan had mentioned her, too. But now Mom skidded away from answering by suggesting that we all go home and think about what had happened.

"We'll decide tomorrow where to go from here," she said.

Luke walked down the hill with J.P. He didn't even look back to see if I was coming.

I tried not to notice. After all, what was he to me? A cute guy who'd made these last few days in Lake Isadora very pleasant. I'd be going home soon. As soon as we could dig information out of my memory—out of *Elaine's* memory—about what had happened to Keith, I would leave Lake Isadora and never come back. Luke had Angelique. Why would he want to hang out with someone who'd discovered that she'd once been his *grandmother*?

Mom was too jazzed up to relax when we got back to our little house.

"I've got to find out where Perla Goudy is," she said.

"Who," I asked again, "is Perla Goudy?"

And again Mom changed the subject, starting to talk about the clothing from the mine. Bud Brady hadn't let Mom take the clothing—Keith's clothing—home with her. He said they had to keep it as evidence of something or other.

But she talked about it, remembering where she'd bought the T-shirt, that the shorts had been mended on the leg where Keith had torn them a little. She dug out her albums and located a photo in which Keith was wearing the sage-green shorts.

"He loved those shorts," she said. "He said they were soft and baggy and didn't itch him anywhere. That's what he said. That they didn't itch him."

It was almost as if she were talking to herself.

I didn't remember having seen the picture before. I'd never had any great curiosity about my missing brother, probably because I was so jealous of him and the way Mom loved him more than she did me.

But I could have seen it and then clothed Keith in those shorts in my mind. Maybe that's why I knew the clothes were his.

No, those memories were *not* imagined. There'd been too many for me to deny them.

But why didn't I have *all* of them then? Why were they so skimpily dealt out to me, so that I had just fragments and nothing to complete a picture? If I'd been reborn as Keith's sister in order to find him, then why couldn't I remember what I really needed to know?

I had to talk to Mariah again.

Or maybe I had to talk to Jonathan.

I waited until Mom finally drifted off to sleep, still holding the album with the picture of Keith in his favorite shorts. Then I headed back up the hill again to Jonathan's house, listening to the whoo-whoo of the mourning doves as the twilight shadows lengthened across the lake in the distance. I hoped I wouldn't meet Luke on the way. Or J.P., either, who had such a problem facing the unchanging loss of the Lion King, along with all his other losses.

I wished I could fix things for him.

I wished I could fix things for me.

eleven

Jonathan was alone when I got to the house on top of the hill. He was in the kitchen, stirring something that smelled warm and chocolatey. In the background I could hear music playing. Something classical. *Four Seasons,* I think. Vivaldi. My grandmother played it a lot.

"Hello, Carlene," Jonathan said, as if it were no surprise that I would come back there. He smiled at me.

"Carlene?" I said. "Aren't you going to call me Elaine? You did once, you know."

He looked up from his stirring. "Do you mean once upon a time when you were Elaine, or once when I first met you as Carlene?"

"Whichever," I said.

"You're not Elaine," he said. "You're Carlene."

Now I was confused. "You *called* me Elaine."

He nodded. "I was given a glimpse. For just a flash I recognized Elaine. I can't explain it." He smiled again as he continued stirring. "Luke thought I was just being barmy again. He thinks I'm beginning to lose it."

I remembered Luke warning me that his grandfather might be a little strange.

I didn't know what to say. I watched him stir for a moment or two, enjoying the smell of the thick pudding that was cooking. I knew what it was now. That good chocolate pudding that I—that *Elaine*—had loved so much. Comfort food, she'd always called it.

"How does it work?" I asked. "I mean, I don't really understand what you're saying. This stuff about my having lived a life as Elaine. A life before this one."

He paused in his stirring for a moment, lifting the spoon, which came up thickly coated with chocolate. "It's time to put in the vanilla," I said. "I never cook it past this stage or it goes to sugar. You don't want to overcook it."

Without saying anything, Jonathan removed the pot from the stove and took a bottle of vanilla extract from a shelf. As he did, I realized what had happened. I'd slipped back into that past life once more. For a moment I'd been Elaine again. I knew because I'd never in my life—in my life as Carlene—made chocolate pudding except the instant stuff you get from a box.

Jonathan measured the vanilla, stirred it into the chocolate, then poured the pudding into four brown stoneware bowls.

I made those bowls. Made them on my potter's wheel and fired them in the kiln in the backyard.

My legs felt rubbery and I stumbled over to a kitchen chair to sit down.

Still holding the hot pot, Jonathan looked over at me, his face concerned. "Are you all right, Elaine?" he asked.

"No," I said. "I'm not all right. And I'm not Elaine. I'm Carlene."

Quickly he put the pot in the sink and came over to sit on a chair beside me. "I'm sorry," he said. "That was clumsy of me. Forgive me. But for just a moment. . . ."

"I know. Every now and then I *am* Elaine." I put my hands over my face, trying to think. "I don't know what's happening. It was so real. I made those bowls, didn't I?"

"No," Jonathan said firmly. "*Elaine* made them."

I took my hands away from my face to look at him. "I could almost feel the clay and the wheel turning, and I was shaping the bowls. I've never even seen a potter's wheel, except in movies. What's happening to me, Jonathan?"

Slowly he shook his head. "I don't know." After thinking for a moment he said, "Do you use a computer?"

"A computer? Yes, sure. Why?"

"Think about it for a moment," he said. "It has a memory in which it stores the information that makes it operate. But it can also store other information. Vast amounts of information, if you've got a big enough hard disk. By clicking on the right files, you can bring any of that information up on your monitor."

I nodded.

"Now think about your brain. Much more complex than a computer. Its capabilities go far beyond a computer. If a machine can store vast amounts of information, think of what the brain can store."

I stared silently at him.

"To get your computer to bring up what you want, you press the right keys. Or manipulate the mouse, or whatever. There are things that trigger the brain to bring up certain memories, too. Like sights. Sounds. Smells. You came into this room where Elaine once lived. You heard her favorite music from the CD player. You smelled her favorite food cooking."

"I became her," I finished. "But why?"

"Have you talked with Mariah about this?" Jonathan asked.

"Yes. She told me about past lives. About being born again to finish some unfinished business, or to achieve some purpose."

"And what purpose were you born again to achieve?" Jonathan prodded.

"To find my lost brother. Elaine was the last person to see him. She must know something that I'm supposed to remember. So we're back to my having been born to find Keith. Why isn't it enough that I was born to live my *own* life?"

"You'll get to do that, Carlene." Jonathan stood up. "I don't understand much better than you do, but what Mariah says makes sense. Some people here think she's pretty weird to believe what she does. But maybe we should go with it. Explore it. *Use* it."

I thought about it. "My computer can import information from other computers through the modem," I said. "Maybe my brain is tapping into memories that are out there in the universe somewhere. Memories that were Elaine's."

"Maybe," Jonathan said.

I shivered although the night was warm. "I just want to be a normal girl. I want to go home. Be with my friends. Go to football games and dances."

Jonathan walked over to look out the window at what was left of the lake in the far distance. "You will," he said. "But think of what this could mean to your family. To find Keith. Or at least know what happened to him," he added. "It would bring your mother peace of mind. It's a terrible thing to lose someone you love."

I waited for a little while, then asked, "Jonathan, what happened to Elaine? How did she come to drown?"

Without turning around, he shook his head. "I don't know, Carlene. I had a head injury. I don't know what happened. There are a lot of things about that terrible day that I don't remember."

So. Were there two mysteries for me to solve? Or more? Were all of these unknowns somewhere in Elaine's memory?

"Perla told me it was fast," Jonathan said. "She said Elaine didn't suffer."

"Perla Goudy? Mom mentioned her, too. Who is she?"

Before Jonathan could tell me, Luke walked into the room. He stopped when he saw me. I expected him to turn on his heel and walk right back out again.

But he didn't. Instead, he came over to where I sat and took both of my hands, lifting me up to stand beside him. "Carlene," he said. "I have something to tell you."

twelve

I expected Luke to say that he was sorry he'd stalked out of Jonathan's house earlier. I expected him to say he realized now that I was *not* his grandmother, that the whole thing was ridiculous even though I was remembering parts of her life.

But instead he said, "Carlene, your mother has been hurt."

Cold fear made me as rigid as an ice sculpture. "Mom?" I said. "I left her drifting off to sleep at our house. I thought she was going to rest for a while. She seemed so out of it. She wanted me to bring back more memories, but I said I couldn't and didn't want to anyway. I said it was spooky and I was scared." I had the feeling that if I kept talking, I could avoid finding out what had happened.

Luke gripped my hands harder. "She drove her car down by the lake to Perla Goudy's cabin. Maybe she hoped Perla was there and went to see her—I don't know. I don't even know if Perla's in town right now. She doesn't come here a whole lot. Anyway, your mother walked out on the big rocks. She fell."

I sucked in air. "How bad is she hurt?"

His eyes didn't waver from mine. "She's unconscious, Carlene. I'll take you to the hospital."

Jonathan erupted in a flurry of activity, checking the stove, throwing the bowls of pudding into the refrigerator, grabbing his car keys. "I'll go, too," he said. "I'll drive, Luke. You take care of Carlene."

Did I need taking care of?

I guess I did. I was trembling, and my mind seemed as frozen as my body. I let Luke guide me out to Jonathan's car where I got into the back seat. He crawled in beside me, still holding one of my hands.

I was glad he was there, warm and solid and comforting.

Jonathan had driven us all the way down the hill before I asked, "Who *is* Perla Goudy? Why would my mom go to her place?"

From the driver's seat, Jonathan glanced briefly over his shoulder. "Perla is—what shall I say? Kind of a fortune-teller. She's always claimed to be psychic. People used to go to her to find out things."

Now what he'd said earlier made sense. He'd said Perla told him Elaine hadn't suffered. That it had been

107

fast, when she drowned. So he had gone to see her, too. And my mom had mentioned her. Maybe she'd consulted Perla about Keith after he'd disappeared. Is that why she'd gone there tonight? Because I'd refused to bring back more of Elaine's memories?

"Can Perla really tell you things that have happened?" I asked Jonathan.

"Sometimes it seems as if she could," Jonathan said. "I don't know for sure. Never did make sense to me, but when you're desperate you'll seek any kind of help."

My mom had been desperate. Maybe if I'd tried to access more of Elaine's memories, maybe if I'd stayed with her, maybe if I'd been more sympathetic, Mom wouldn't have gone to Perla's place and slipped on the rocks.

I turned to Luke. "Who found my mom? Did someone see her fall?"

He nodded. "Yes. Davy Van Dyke. If he hadn't, she could have drowned."

Jonathan turned his head to look back at Luke. "Davy? Is he . . ." He hesitated, then finished, ". . . in town?"

"Yes." Luke glanced at me and didn't say anything more.

Neither did I. I was too disturbed about Mom to do more than wonder briefly if this was the same guy

Mom said had been in jail, and if he could possibly have done something there at the lake to hurt her.

Mom looked pale and diminished in her hospital bed. Her eyes were closed. There was an IV attached to her hand and an oxygen tube in her nose.

"Mom," I whispered.

She didn't respond.

I turned to the nurse who stood by my side. "Can she hear me?"

"I don't know," the nurse said. "But it's good to talk to her. She might be hearing it."

I took Mom's limp hand. "Mom, I'm here. I'll stay here until you're better. Come back, Mom. We have to find Keith."

It was then that I vowed that whatever I had to do, I would do. I would dig down into my brain to find Elaine's memories, I would go where familiar things might trigger the memories as they had at Jonathan's house. Seeing Mom lying there made me understand a little of what Jonathan had said about how losing someone you love makes you desperate. I loved my mom. I would do anything to help her.

Luke and Jonathan waited at the hospital with me until late that night. Mom still hadn't awakened, so they took me off to the cafeteria where they made sure

I ate something. "We don't want you collapsing, too," Jonathan said.

While we ate, I told them what I'd decided. "I want to go to the lake," I said. "I want to walk along the shore, and I want to take a boat out to where the accident happened. I'll take my binoculars so I can look all around and see if any more memories come back to me."

Jonathan gave me that gentle, sweet look that was now becoming familiar. "You want to see what Elaine saw," he said.

I nodded. "I want to *be* Elaine during those last moments of her life," I said.

"You're a brave girl," Jonathan said, and Luke reached out to cover my hand with his own.

"Tomorrow," I said. "Can we go out on the lake tomorrow?"

Both Luke and Jonathan nodded. "We can take my boat," Jonathan said.

I stayed with Mom at the hospital that night, sleeping in a chair beside her bed. She didn't awaken. She didn't respond at all when I told her what I was going to do the next day. I thought if she could hear me, it might alarm her enough to bring her back from wherever she was. But she was silent and unresponsive.

Mariah came before I left the next morning. "I'll stay

with her today, Carlene," she said. "You go home and get some rest."

I thought about telling her my plans. She might have some suggestions to help me find those memories that must be locked somewhere in my brain. Maybe she could tell me more that I needed to know about past lives.

On the other hand, she might talk me out of going on the lake today. She might say to let things just come back by themselves. I didn't really know *what* she would say about it. So I didn't tell her what I was going to do.

I called Luke to say I was ready to go. He came to the hospital to take me home to change my clothes and pick up my binoculars. Then we went to get Jonathan.

At his house, we found that he'd fixed breakfast for us. "You're not going out there on an empty stomach," he told me.

"Maybe it would be better if I'm a little weak," I said. "I mean, maybe that would help Elaine to take over."

Jonathan looked sharply at me as he slid a large pancake from the griddle onto a plate. "You're not a split personality, Carlene. It's not like you're inviting Elaine to take over your body. You're not trying to go into a trance or anything like that. All you want to do is tap into her memories. You can do that just as well when you've eaten." He put the plate on the table and waved a hand at a chair.

I smiled at him. "It smells delicious."

I sat down where he indicated and poured syrup over the pancake, surprised that I was suddenly quite hungry.

"There's pudding for dessert," Jonathan said as he put out plates for him and Luke. "We didn't get to eat it yesterday."

The chocolate comfort pudding, Elaine's favorite food. Couldn't hurt to have some of that. The smell of it had triggered her memories yesterday.

"I never had dessert for breakfast before," I said.

"One of life's great pleasures," Jonathan said with a smile.

"J.P. wanted to come with us." Luke sat down and began to eat. "He was already at the newspaper office when I got there, and of course he wanted to know where I was going. I just told him that I had to go out on the lake."

"He loves the lake," Jonathan said. He, too, sat down to eat. "How did you get him to stay at the office?"

Luke grinned. "I said I had a deadline to meet this afternoon, an article to finish for this week's edition . . . which is the truth. I told him I wasn't going to have time to go to the library and ask his aunt Fran for books about the old hotel that was moved when the dam was built. He said he'd be glad to go get them for me and have them waiting when I get back."

"He's a sweet little guy," I said around a big bite of pancake. *Jonathan always made the pancakes. They were his specialty.*

It jolted me a little to have a memory appear at that moment. But that was good, wasn't it? Elaine was there, waiting.

I didn't mention that the memory had come. I was afraid talking too much about Elaine might distance her from me on the day when I wanted especially for her to come through.

"Yeah, J.P. is a neat kid," Luke said.

And Jonathan said, "He's a lot like Keith was, friendly and outgoing. Curious. Helpful. Interested in everything."

"The kind of kid everyone would like to have," I said. "Maybe somebody liked Keith enough to steal him away."

"Maybe." Jonathan skated a piece of pancake around his plate to sop up the last of the syrup, then put his fork down. "But who?"

That was the question I hoped to solve that day.

The chocolate pudding we ate while we laughed

about the decadence of having dessert for breakfast didn't bring back any more of Elaine's memories.

The day was all brilliant sunshine and blue sky, and the water of the lake was calm as we sped out in Jonathan's shiny new motorboat. Jonathan said the boat he and Elaine had been in on the day of the accident had been a rowboat, but Luke said we could cover more ground, so to speak, in a motorboat.

Luke pointed out the rocks where Mom had fallen.

"Could she have been looking for—something?" I asked.

Jonathan shook his head. "The accident was way over there by the cliffs where the water is still deep." He paused for what seemed like a long time. "But the rocks—that's where Elaine's body was found. The rocks were underneath the water at that time."

I shivered. Why hadn't some kind of memory come up when we'd passed the rocks?

I raised my binoculars and looked back at the rocks, afraid of remembering something awful but hoping some memory would come anyway.

There was nothing.

Aiming my binoculars at the hill behind the rocks, I looked past the stumps of dead trees that had been underwater for all those years, then farther up to the live pines that stood beside a run-down cabin.

Perla's cabin. Perla, who didn't live there anymore.

But then who was standing there under one of the tall pines, one hand shading a face turned toward us as we sped across the lake?

I wondered, without any real reason to think so, if it might be Davy Van Dyke.

thirteen

Quickly I handed the binoculars to Jonathan. "Look," I said. "Someone's there."

He took the glasses and lifted them to his eyes, scanning the area around Perla Goudy's old cabin. "Where? I don't see anybody."

From his place behind the steering wheel of the boat, Luke craned his neck to look back at the shore. "Sure it isn't a shadow?"

I pointed. "I'm sure. It's a person, right there under the tall trees." Squinting, I tried to see. But even without the binoculars I couldn't see anybody there. "I guess whoever it was left."

"Was it a woman or a man?" Jonathan asked.

"I couldn't tell. He—she—was dressed in jeans and a plaid shirt. I don't know if it was a man or a woman."

Jonathan raised the binoculars again. "There was someone watching that other time," he said so softly that I could barely hear him over the buzz of the boat's motor.

And suddenly I was in another time. *I was hanging on to the sides of a pitching boat with Jonathan at the oars. Someone stood back there under the trees by Perla's cabin, watching. I waved frantically, trying to signal that we were in trouble. The person turned and ran back toward the cabin. I didn't see him—or her—again.*

"Perla," I whispered. "Get help."

Suddenly Perla was there in my mind, small, a little overweight, dressed in flowing, gauzy skirts and gypsy-bright blouses. I remembered her. Or *Elaine* remembered her.

Jonathan lowered the glasses to look at me. He didn't say anything, but I guess he knew from my face that I'd remembered something else.

"Could have been anybody," Luke said. "Kids like to go there and snoop around. It's the local haunted house."

"*Is* it haunted?" I asked.

Luke shrugged. "Who knows? I guess every town needs an old house where the kids can terrorize one another. Perla's cabin is ours. We used to call it 'the witch's house.'"

"You thought Perla was a witch?" I asked.

"She went away before I was born," Luke said. "But people still talked about her, the way she told fortunes

117

and made predictions and stuff like that. We kids translated that as 'witch.' She was probably a very nice lady."

"What happened to her?" I asked. "Perla, I mean."

Jonathan handed the binocs back to me. "She left town not too long after Elaine and I were married. She got married herself a little later and went to live in Tehachapi or somewhere near there. She's been divorced for years but still stays there to be close to her kids. Or kid—I think she had only one. She comes down now and then to check on her cabin."

My mom wanted to find Perla. She'd probably been looking for her when she fell on the rocks.

Thinking about Mom lying so pale and still on her hospital bed made me wonder how she was.

"Maybe we'd better go back," I said. "I don't seem to be getting any more memories about what happened here."

"We're almost there," Jonathan said. "Where the accident happened. Where I was injured. I don't know what happened after that and don't remember a whole lot before." He squinted in the direction we were heading. "I don't even know how I came to be hurt," he added. "I lost almost all my memories of that day."

But Elaine knew. And that's why we were here. To see if Elaine could give me more clues about what happened to her . . . and to Jonathan . . . and to Keith.

My stomach lurched as the churning water tossed the

boat, and my breath came in gasps as I reached out for Keith's small hand.

"Closer," I panted. "Jonathan! Just a little closer."

Keith's face was terrified, and I kept my eyes locked on his, trying to give him some kind of assurance and comfort. Our hands touched for a fraction of a second, but then the other boat moved away.

"Keith," I screamed. "Here, grab my hand."

He leaned toward me, dangerously close to falling out. But the boat he was on pulled farther away from ours.

With a start, I came back to the present.

"It was the same scene as I saw before," I said. "I already know that part of what happened."

Jonathan reached up from the back seat to take my hand. "Maybe there's some reason to see it again. Was there anything new that you didn't see before?"

I shook my head.

Jonathan pointed toward the shore. "This is it," he said. "This is where we tried to get Keith. I remember the big tree over there." I looked ahead to the craggy shore where a gnarled old live oak spread its knobby limbs. It was a long way from the water now, but that was only because the lake had shrunk so much from the drought.

We were all silent as we looked toward the tree. I closed my eyes, reaching for another memory.

"I'm not getting anything more," I said finally.

Jonathan nodded slowly. "Let's go back, Luke," he said. "We'll come here again on another day, but we'd better go check on Carlene's mother now."

Luke swung the boat in a wide arc, and with a roar we started back toward the dock.

I was relieved. The visions scared me. The fact that I had Elaine's memories somewhere in my brain scared me. Being there on the lake scared me.

But what scared me most was the sudden realization as I looked back at the old tree that there *had* been something new in what I'd seen today. I knew now why the scene had been replayed. It was to tell me that the boat Keith was in had deliberately moved away from Jonathan and Elaine. *Away!*

I closed my eyes, straining to see the face of that man, trying to see past the yellow plastic rain hat. I pleaded silently. *I'm so close to knowing, Elaine. Give me that scene one more time and let me see the face.*

"What's the matter, Carlene?" Jonathan asked. "Are you sick?"

I realized I'd bent forward on my seat and put my head in my hands. I straightened up, turning to look back at Jonathan.

"Yes, maybe." I told him about my realization that the boat carrying Keith had purposely moved away from the one he and Elaine had been in.

Now it was Jonathan's turn to look sick. "I *remem-*

ber," he said. "Oh, I remember!" His voice sounded hoarse and whispery as he went on. "I remember rowing faster, thinking it was just the water that was taking them away. I tried to get close to them, yelling for the guy to stop, to try to turn toward us. We got very close, and . . ." His face contorted with pain. "If only I could remember what happened next. But I guess that's when I got the head injury."

Luke cut the engine and let the boat drift gently on the waves. "How did you get to shore, Grandpa?"

Jonathan's eyes seemed to look into the past. "I found out later that when Carl Carter got out from under the boat where he'd been trapped, he swam over to my boat and brought us both in. But Elaine was gone. Keith, too."

I thought how very bizarre this whole thing was and how difficult it must be for Jonathan. He'd come back to the place where his wife had died, and I was there with her memories invading my mind, yet I wasn't her. But, according to Mariah, I had once lived as her and now was back as somebody else to remember what had happened on that dreadful day.

I hoped something good would eventually come out of this nightmare.

J.P. met us at the dock. "Your mom is awake," he told me. "She wants you to come." He took my hand, carefully holding away his thumb with the warts on it so I wouldn't have to touch them. He was barefoot, as usual, but today he wore a tan T-shirt with his shorts. The ever-present necktie with its neat knot was there around his neck.

"How did you get here?" I asked. It was too far for him to walk around the lake to the dock.

"Mariah brought me," he said. "She left me with Hal, the dock dude, and told me to tell you to hurry to the hospital as soon as you came back with the boat."

My heart began to thud. "Why do I need to hurry?"

J.P. shrugged. "Just because your mom is awake, I guess."

"Is she okay?"

He shrugged again. "I didn't see her. That's all Mariah told me."

"I'm sure she's all right, Carlene," Jonathan said. We were back at the car now and he opened the door so we could all get inside. "I'm sure she's just anxious to see you."

"I'm sure, too," I said. But I wasn't sure at all. Bad things *could* happen. However, if she was awake, that must mean she'd be all right.

J.P. seemed permanently attached to me, so he and I got into the back seat. I appreciated the warm comfort of his small, warty hand. He knew all about losing a mother.

He waved to Hal, the dock dude, as we pulled away. I listened to the crunch of the tires on the gravel road, which ran along the dry shore of the lake, and tried not to think.

"Knock knock," J.P. said.

Knock-knock jokes were the last thing I wanted to hear at that moment, but I said automatically, "Who's there?"

"Freddie."

"Freddie who?"

"Freddie or not, here I come," J.P. said with a grin.

I didn't say anything.

"You know," he said. "Like when you're playing hide-and-seek."

"I know, J.P. It's a good joke."

"I just wanted to cheer you up, Carlene," he said anxiously.

I squeezed his hand and smiled. "It did cheer me, J.P. Thanks."

He sat beside me in comforting silence until we got to the hospital.

We all went in. The admitting nurse was about to tell J.P. to remain in the waiting room, but I gripped his hand and said that it was important for him to be with me. She didn't object.

I took a deep breath before I walked through the open door of Mom's room.

She was still lying flat in the bed, but her eyes were open now. There was a woman standing beside the bed, a small woman who wore blue jeans and a plaid shirt. I knew immediately that she was the person who'd been at the cabin by the lake, the one I'd seen through my binoculars. I also knew that even though she wasn't wearing the kind of clothes I remembered—*Elaine* remembered—that she was Perla Goudy.

Mom raised a weak hand in greeting. "Carlene," she said, "something wonderful has happened. Perla is here, and she's going to help you get to Elaine's memories about Keith."

fourteen

For just a moment I let Elaine's memories of Perla sit there in my mind. It was clear to me that Elaine had known Perla. Something was not quite right. Nothing frightening. Maybe watchful. I couldn't really identify the feeling.

"Hello, Mrs. Goudy," I said.

Perla stared intently at me. I had the sensation that she was probing beneath the surface, snooping around in the mechanisms of my brain. Maybe it was because of her eyes, which were deep-brown and so brilliant that they seemed to pierce right through my skull.

She gave me a slight smile. "Call me Perla," she said. "You always did before, Elaine."

"My name is Carlene," I said.

"Of course," she said. "I'm sorry. Your mother told me what's been happening. The memories."

As I stood there uncertain of what to do, Perla looked behind me.

"Jonathan," she said softly.

I turned to see Jonathan nod stiffly at her. "Perla," he said. "It's been a long time."

"Yes." Her eyes lasered him. "You're well?" she asked.

"I am."

Something about their exchange of words made me wonder what had happened between them in the past. There was some kind of history, that was certain. Did Elaine know about it? Was that why I felt that she was wary of Perla?

No more memories surfaced.

I'd almost forgotten that Luke and J.P. were there, too. They stood slightly behind and off to the side of Jonathan.

Perla gazed at Luke. "This has to be your grandson, Jonathan," she said. "He looks a lot like you did when you were his age."

"I'm Luke, ma'am," Luke said politely. "You're right. I'm his grandson."

Perla nodded. "And who is this?" Her brilliant eyes examined J.P., who reached out a hand to grasp Luke's.

"I'm Justin Paul Eddington," J.P. said firmly. I'd never heard him use his full name before. In fact, I hadn't even known what the J.P. stood for until now.

"Eddington," Perla said. "Of course." She said it as if

she knew all about J.P. Then she turned back to look at Mom. "I'll set up an appointment, Jen, as soon as you get out of the hospital."

Mom's face drooped. "Can't we do it today, Perla? Here?"

Perla shook her head. "It's not that easy, Jen. You know that. And a hospital is not the right place for a regression."

A regression? I hadn't heard that word before. I wasn't quite sure what it meant, but I knew it involved me. And Elaine.

Mom was clearly disappointed. "We're so close, Perla. I know now that Keith's alive. If we can just find out what Elaine saw, we'll be able to trace him."

Perla put out a hand to pat Mom on the shoulder. "I hope so, Jen. I hope so."

She turned to go then, looking at each of us as she passed and murmuring her good-byes. She smiled at J.P. and reached out to touch his arm.

He sidled closer to Luke but didn't say anything until we heard her retreating footsteps die away. Then he said, "She makes me feel like Hansel."

All of us looked at him, puzzled.

"Hansel?" Luke echoed.

J.P. nodded. "*You* know. Like in *Hansel and Gretel*, when the witch keeps looking at Hansel to see if he's fat enough to cook."

I was so startled I was sure Elaine would have some reaction, but that wasn't the way it worked. Elaine wasn't lurking there in my head, listening to what was said. She was dead, and I, who supposedly had lived her life, carried only fragments of her memories. I had no clue as to what triggered them to come forward when they did. But from what I could determine from those memories, Elaine had known Perla and although she didn't totally like her, I didn't feel she'd been afraid of her.

So it would be up to me to figure out what part Perla had played in past events. And not only what Elaine knew about Keith's disappearance, but also what Perla knew.

It was easy to see that Mom was exhausted after Perla left. Her face was as pale as the bandages around her head, and reaching her hand out to take mine seemed to be a major effort, but she looked happy.

"It's all coming together, Carlene," she said. "We'll make an appointment with Perla as soon as I get out of here. She'll be able to regress you back to Elaine's memories."

Regress. There was that word again. Part of me shrank away from even asking what it meant. Besides, it was time for Mom to rest. It had been just a couple of hours since she'd regained consciousness.

"We'll talk about it later," I told her.

A brisk nurse in a brightly flowered smock came into the room with a tray of medications, giving us a good excuse to leave.

"I'll come back tonight, Mom," I said as J.P., Luke, Jonathan, and I filed out into the corridor.

We walked along silently, peering now and then through an open door at patients inside the rooms. Some lay sleeping. Others chatted with visitors. One man who sat upright watching TV waved at us. "Come back soon," he called with a grin.

"We will, Ed," Jonathan said. "Get yourself well."

This was a small town. Of course Jonathan would know almost everybody.

"How well do you know Perla?" I blurted.

He hesitated just a moment before saying, "Well enough. We've known each other since we were kids. Her name was Pett then, before she was married. Perla Pett."

He didn't seem too eager to say more, but I went on. "Can she really do this—whatever it is Mom wants her to do?"

"Regression," Jonathan said. "Are you asking is she qualified?"

I wasn't sure what I was asking since I didn't know what regression was. "Yes," I said. "I guess that's what I mean."

Again Jonathan paused. "It's a thing Perla does.

129

She's always had a leaning toward that kind of thing." He hesitated, then said, "Carlene, I'd rather you talk to a trained hypnotherapist. Somebody who's studied psychology and the workings of the mind. Somebody who doesn't know everything that's happened in this town."

So what was he saying?

I didn't have a chance to ask because we'd reached the front door by then and suddenly come face to face with Angelique, who was coming into the hospital.

I must admit that I'd almost forgotten she existed. I'd more or less absorbed Luke into the group of people I needed to help me through this whole thing. I needed him there with me, just as I needed Jonathan and J.P. It didn't seem to bother him anymore that in a previous life I'd apparently been his grandmother. I was grateful for that.

Angelique's eyes slid from Luke to me, veered to Jonathan and J.P., then fastened on me. I expected her to make some kind of accusation, to demand that I stay away from her guy, to cut me down with some kind of nasty remark. But all she said was, "I hear that your mother is feeling better, Carlene. You must have been really worried."

I hadn't even been aware that she knew my name.

My mouth must have dropped open. "I was," I squeaked.

"She'll be okay now," Angelique said, touching my arm as she went on into the hospital. "See you tonight, Luke," she called over her shoulder. "Seven? My house?"

"Seven's fine," Luke said.

Okay, so she wasn't going to miss a chance after all to remind me that I was trespassing.

"She volunteers here," Luke said as we continued on toward Jonathan's car. "Her dad is a doctor, and she wants to be one someday."

So her evaluation of my mom had probably been like a professional courtesy rather than any move toward friendship. That was okay with me, but my heart did a little flip-flop as I realized that I was no match for Angelique, who wanted to be a doctor. What did I want? Just to get back to my old home in Arletta and be with my friends. No, there was more to me than that. I wanted to make my mom happy. I wanted to find my long-lost brother. My families-are-forever brother. I did have a goal after all. Beyond that? It seemed enough for now.

"Tell me about regression," I said to Jonathan as we all climbed into his car. Luke drove, with Jonathan in the passenger seat. J.P., as before, got into the back seat with me, a comforting presence.

"Well," Jonathan said. "It's not like I understand it myself. In this case the therapist would take you back to Elaine's memories through hypnotism or suggestion.

You'd be in a completely relaxed state, which would help you to remember."

"Is Perla a therapist?" I asked.

Jonathan shook his head. "Like I said, she's just had a leaning toward that sort of thing. A natural ability."

"I don't want her messing with me," I said. "With Elaine."

"I'll see if I can get in touch with Neil Ostergard," Jonathan said. "He was my college roommate a long time ago. He's a psychologist. He could tell us the right way to do this."

"I'd really appreciate it," I said. "Mom is so determined that I'm afraid she'll force me to go to Perla. There must be some other way."

Luke wasn't saying anything. He was probably thinking of what he and Angelique were going to do that night. Was there a movie house in town? A spot to dance? A nice place to eat? Other than Ivy's Eats, that is. Maybe a place with dim lights and soft music where a young couple could whisper together and exchange a kiss or two. Overlooking the lake maybe. Some place that a girl would write about in her diary.

Why had a diary suddenly come to mind? Had Elaine taken me there?

"Jonathan," I said. "Did Elaine keep diaries?"

He nodded. "A whole shelf of them. Seems like she was always writing in one."

"I have to see them," I said. "Can we go back to your house right now? I need to read them."

He turned to look at me. "Good idea, Carlene. But are you sure you're up to it? Reading about a life that you apparently lived could be disturbing."

How could *anyone* be up to such a thing? But the stakes were high. I was willing to do anything that might give us even the faintest clue about what happened.

"Yes," I said. "I want to read the diaries."

fifteen

All the way to Jonathan's house, J.P. tried to coax Luke to take him out on the lake. He promised everything from shining Luke's shoes every day ("I wear sneakers all the time," Luke said) to giving him three of his best baseball cards, if he'd just take him for a boat ride.

"You taught me all about lifesaving," J.P. said. "So if the boat tips over, I can save you."

Luke seemed preoccupied as he drove—was he thinking of Angelique?—but he turned his head to grin at J.P. "Patience, pal," he said. "I'll take you out as soon as I have time."

"I know all about 'as soon as,'" J.P. grumbled. "That's what everybody always says, but 'as soon as' never comes."

"We'll see if we can make 'as soon as' come as soon as I finish the story I'm doing for Mariah," Luke said.

J.P. sighed and settled back to examine the wart on his right hand. "My mom said she'd be back as soon as she got her head together, but she's still gone." He looked down at his necktie, and I wondered for the hundredth time what it meant to him and why he wouldn't go anywhere without it.

I put my arm around him. "Why is it you want to go out on the lake, J.P.?"

He was silent for a moment. "I just want to, that's all," he said finally.

Luke glanced over his shoulder, giving me an "I'll tell you later" look.

We were at Jonathan's house on the hill by then. Luke stopped the car and we all got out. "There are some M&M's on the kitchen table that you can have as soon as we get inside," he told J.P. "There's one 'as soon as' that's going to happen."

J.P. sprinted on ahead.

"Last time he saw his mother was on the lake," Luke whispered to me when he was out of earshot. "She went off in a big boat with her new guy. He's never said so, but I think he figures she'll come back the same way."

"Poor little guy." I kept walking steadily toward the door, but my heart thudded dully. We were there to look at Elaine's diaries, and I was nervous. It was late afternoon by then, and the setting sun caused the oak trees and tall pines to cast long shadows that seemed to reach out toward the house. Mourning doves whoo-whooed from the canyons below us, and the evening cricket concert was just beginning.

There was a dreamlike quality to everything. The mountains, which stretched as far as we could see, were blue and misty. The far distant lake, almost hidden now that it had shrunk so much, was slightly blurred by the fading light, like a smudgy charcoal drawing. I had the odd thought that the lake was like Elaine, offering merely a glimpse now and then of what it once had been.

Even the sound of our footsteps on Jonathan's bare hardwood floors was echoing and unreal. It all seemed to fit in with the eerie idea that I was here to read about a life I'd once lived but now remembered only fragments of.

J.P. was already sitting at the kitchen table, picking all the red M&M's from a bowl. Luke went straight to the telephone and called Mariah, telling her he'd got tied up with something but that he'd turn in his already overdue article the next day. Then he called J.P.'s aunt Fran to let her know where J.P. was. "I'll bring him home about six-thirty," he said.

Six-thirty. Leaving enough time for Luke to shower before his date with Angelique.

I wished he'd say something about that date—just mention where they were going, maybe. But of course it was none of my business. I was the outsider here, the interloper. Luke probably just hung out with me because he was curious about what was going on with all the stuff about Keith. Or maybe he planned to do a scoop for the newspaper when we found out anything. Maybe he even planned to get into the big time with a story for the *Los Angeles Times,* or some other major city paper. A story like mine could take him a long way toward becoming a recognized journalist, even though he was young.

Jonathan was opening a glass-fronted bookcase in the big kitchen. It was filled with notebooks, file folders, and boxes. The notebooks, I assumed, were Elaine's diaries. Why wasn't I recognizing them? If I had lived Elaine's life, why didn't the books look familiar to me? After all, I had written them. Or Elaine had written them when I was her. Or when she'd occupied my body. No, not my body. She'd had a different body.

It was so confusing that it made my head ache to think about it. So I just watched as Jonathan pulled out a black-and-white-speckled composition notebook.

"This is from the fifties," he said, looking at its cover. "She was just a teenager. That's too soon for you to be interested."

"No," I said. "If I'm trying to bring back Elaine's memories, nothing is too early." I reached out for the diary, but then involuntarily withdrew my hand as if I expected it to be hot to the touch.

Jonathan gave me a quizzical look. I forced myself to reach out again and this time took the diary from him.

I wasn't zapped by an electric current when I touched it, nor did it suddenly make me remember. It was just a notebook.

I took it back to the kitchen table where Luke had sat down beside J.P., opening it somewhere near the middle. "'June 15,'" I read. "'School is O-U-T! Hooray! An okay report card.'" I turned to Jonathan. "So Elaine wasn't crazy about school?"

Jonathan grinned. "Nobody's crazy about school by the last day. She liked it all right. She was a good student. An okay report card to her probably meant one B in the midst of a cluster of A's."

I let my mind go blank for a moment to see if anything of Elaine's memories of school would surface.

I wasn't surprised that nothing did. I knew I was still resisting this whole idea that I should look inward and see Elaine.

I flipped through a few pages of the diary, then skipped ahead a couple of months. Elaine had written something for nearly every day. Like an August entry in which she told about Jonathan calling to ask if she'd like to go for an ice cream:

We walked down to Patterson's Parlor. Mrs. Patterson gave us two scoops for the price of one, just because it was a nice day. We walked back and sat on the brick wall to eat our cones. My scoops were chocolate and strawberry. Jonathan's were both vanilla. We traded tastes.

Suddenly I felt very self-conscious, reading my diary in front of Luke and J.P. and Jonathan. No, not *my* diary. Elaine's. But it seemed like an invasion of her privacy to be making it such a public thing. Maybe I should take the diary back to the little house Mom and I shared and read it alone. If it *were* my own diary, I wouldn't be reading it in front of other people.

I closed the notebook.

"Something wrong?" Jonathan asked.

"Reading her diary," I said. "I'm not sure we should be doing it."

I was glad Jonathan didn't rush into reassurances that it was all right. He sat there looking at me for a long moment. Then he said, "Why do people keep diaries?"

I didn't say anything so he went on. "Is it just to help them remember what happened as they go on through the hours and years of their lives? Or is it to tell future generations what it was like to be that particular person on that particular day? Diaries are written for the future, Carlene. It's all right to read them. What is it that bothers you?"

"I'm not sure," I said. "But the day I just read about—I think it was the first of her memories that I received. I don't know why she'd remember that particular day."

I opened the notebook again, found the entry, and showed it to Jonathan.

Sitting down at the table, he read the entry aloud for Luke and J.P.'s benefit.

"Is there something important about that day?" I asked. "Something that should tell me something?"

He considered for a moment, then said, "When you get to be my age you realize that *every* day is important. Just that you're alive is important. But if you're asking if there should be some clue you should know from that day, I'd say no. You probably remembered it because it was summer and Elaine was young and happy." He paused. "It was our first date." He smiled shyly at me.

Luke was grinning. "What did you write in *your* journal, Grandpa?"

"Didn't keep a journal," Jonathan said. "But I'd never forget that day."

J.P. sat with his elbows resting on the kitchen table, munching M&M's. His forehead was furrowed, as if he were thinking hard.

"It was exciting enough just to be with Elaine," Jonathan went on, then actually blushed. "We'd known each other since kindergarten. I thought she was the prettiest girl in the world."

It occurred to me that I had never seen what she looked like. "I'd like to see a picture of her."

Jonathan got up and went over to the bookcase, from

which he took a box that had once held chocolates. Opening it, he picked up a picture, looked at it for a moment, then passed it to me.

It was strange not to recognize a face that Elaine must have looked at thousands of times in her forty-six years. The picture was taken when she was young, maybe in the last years of high school or maybe in college. She'd had dark hair and eyes, and even though the picture was black and white, I could see that her face was tanned and smooth. I could see a resemblance to Luke, but she certainly didn't look a thing like me.

It was ridiculous to think that she *should* look like me, since we weren't related in any way. We'd merely both occupied the same . . . *vehicle.* Even that wasn't strictly accurate.

What we shared was a *soul.*

That made my heart thud because I had no concept of how it could be. What was a soul, anyway? *Where* was it? In my heart? My brain? Did it fit my body like a glove? Or was it inside, filling out all my inner spaces? Was it a patchwork affair, with pieces of Elaine intermingled with pieces of me? And maybe other lives, from somewhere in the distant past?

"Jonathan," J.P. said.

"Yo," Jonathan answered.

"I've been wondering," J.P. said. "How come you got *two* scoops of vanilla?"

I had to backpedal to understand where he was coming from. He was stuck on the ice cream cones.

I laughed. Here I'd been trying to uncover the secrets of the universe while J.P. pondered the wisdom of *two* scoops of vanilla. He dealt strictly with the basics.

Jonathan ruffled his hair. "I liked vanilla best, J.P. Still do."

"You oughta try something new," J.P. commented. "Maybe you'd like it."

Maybe I should try something new, too. Really get into this past-life thing. Stop being afraid of it. Relax, and let it happen.

Maybe I'd like it.

Luke left right after we ate dessert. He offered to drop me off at my house, but I asked Jonathan if I could stay a while. If I was going to shed my reluctance to really pursue Elaine, I might as well get on with it.

J.P. opted to stay, too. Jonathan said he'd take us both home in a little while.

I lost interest in the diary after Luke left. I couldn't concentrate. I kept seeing him and Angelique together, with her clinging possessively to his arm.

Jonathan must have sensed something because he said, "You may take the diaries home with you if you'd like, Carlene. Maybe it *would* be better if you read them alone."

"Thank you, Jonathan," I said. So instead of reading any more, I began flipping through the box of photographs. There were pictures of Elaine in a wide poodle skirt from the fifties, and Elaine in a flowing flower-child dress from the sixties.

I showed that one to Jonathan. Smiling, he said, "We weren't really into that stuff. But she looked terrific in those gauzy dresses." His eyes were tender as he gazed at the photo.

There was a lovely wedding photo of Jonathan, dark and handsome, and Elaine, wearing a cloud of white, standing in front of a pretty white-clapboard church. It wasn't a professional picture, just a snapshot. I knew the church was the one that had been moved when the area was flooded to create the lake. But what caught my eye was the girl on Jonathan's other side. Whereas Elaine merely held Jonathan's hand, this girl was glued to his arm, much the way Angelique held on to Luke's arm. Odd, I thought. Odder still when I realized the girl was Perla. A young Perla, slim and petite. What was the story there? Why would she attach herself to Jonathan on his wedding day?

It seemed too personal to ask, so I went on down through the stack of photos until I came to one of Jonathan and Perla. It was a color picture and must have been somewhat recent, because they looked more like they did now. They stood looking down at

J.P., who was showing them something he held in his hands.

But as I looked at the picture, I realized it wasn't J.P. at all. This picture was taken many years before he was born. The boy was Keith.

Immediately I was back there in that time and place.

I knew Jonathan and Perla were not aware of my presence. I'd gone to get my camera from the car to take pictures of the sunset over the lake. I don't know where Perla came from, although I knew she'd been visiting from her home up north. She was there beside Jonathan, and Keith Carter was with them. I didn't see his parents, but they must have been close by.

There was something charming about the way Jonathan and Perla bent over to look at whatever Keith was showing them, so I snapped a picture.

I was sure they must have heard the snick of the camera, but maybe not since Perla suddenly put her arm through Jonathan's and wrapped the other one around Keith.

"Isn't this perfect?" she said. "Just the three of us?"

The scene ended as suddenly as it had begun and I was left knowing why Elaine felt wary of Perla, who had apparently wanted to be more to Jonathan than she should.

"I'd like to go home now, Jonathan," I said. "Do you have a box for the diaries?"

I was ready to read them through and let Elaine lead me where she would.

sixteen

Jonathan delivered J.P. to his aunt Fran before driving me home. I watched as he escorted the boy inside, wondering as I'd done a dozen times before why J.P. never took off the ratty necktie that dangled down across his chest.

I asked Jonathan about it when he returned to the car. "Luke says J.P. won't talk about it," I said. "I was thinking maybe you would know when he started wearing it. Or at least where he got it."

"Was his dad's." Jonathan settled behind the steering wheel and shifted into gear. "Don't know that he even remembers his dad. He skipped when the boy was only about three years old."

"So how do you know the necktie belonged to him?"

"Saw him wear it," Jonathan said.

I raised my eyebrows. "You remember a necktie from that long ago?"

Now it was his turn to raise his eyebrows. "Long ago? Four years?"

For someone who was over sixty, four years probably didn't amount to much. To me it seemed like a long time. To J.P. it would be more than half his life.

So time wasn't the same to everybody.

I filed that thought away, feeling that it was significant.

Jonathan was still speaking. "It's a tie you don't forget," he said. "Especially when Riley called attention to it every time he wore it, which wasn't often. Riley, that's J.P.'s dad."

I closed my eyes, trying for an image of the grungy necktie. I hadn't paid that much attention to what was on it, but when I concentrated I remembered a mountain scene with a lake in front and a tiny fisherman on the shore, casting his line out across the water.

"Was he a fisherman?" I asked. "Riley, I mean?"

Jonathan nodded as he turned the car into the driveway of the little house my mother and I were renting. "Fisherman. Hunter. Mountain man. Got tired of holding down a job and took off. The necktie is probably all J.P. has left of him."

"How about his mother? What was she like? Why did she leave?"

Jonathan ran a hand through his graying hair. "Craved excitement, Maxine did. Changed her name to Capri early on. Liked to party. Didn't take to child care. She left right soon after Riley did. Don't think she left even as much as a necktie for J.P. Just a promise that she'd be back 'soon.'"

I remembered J.P. asking how soon "soon" was.

"Whole town took him over after they left. Reckon it saved him from becoming too messed up."

That wasn't the way Jonathan used to talk. He was a teacher. His speech was always smooth and articulate.

The thought was there in my head as if I'd known Jonathan for a long time.

Elaine had known Jonathan for a long time. So was this older Jonathan, gray-haired and terse, as much a stranger to her as he was to me? Was she there inside me listening to everything that went on?

No, I had figured that out before. She wasn't there like a roommate inside my body. I had some of her memories, and it was only logical, if anything about this was logical, that the memories would tell me he was different as a young man. Or just my own common sense would say that it was unusual for a person who had spent his working life as a teacher to lapse into a casual pattern of speech now and then.

But time and experiences changed people. Keith would be changed, if he was alive. He'd be twenty-two now, not the little boy Mom had lost.

It occurred to me that perhaps he, wherever he was,

needed help and that was what had started the memories coming to me. There had to be a reason. Maybe he was trying to reach out to his family, his forever-family, through me.

I put my questions on hold as Jonathan carried the box containing Elaine's diaries inside the house, then left.

I was alone with my thoughts—and Elaine's diaries.

Spreading the diaries out on the kitchen table, I tried to get a handle on this time thing that had occurred to me earlier. It seemed as if the longer a person lived, the faster time passed and the more closely connected the events of a life were. One thing was the seed of the next.

Maybe I should remember *that* as I read through the diaries. Perhaps I would discover some seeds that would be whole fruit by now, and Jonathan, to whom four years, even fourteen, nineteen, twenty, were not all that long ago, could make some connections.

Keith had supposedly drowned eighteen years ago. I was fifteen now. To me, it was impossible to relate something that happened before I was even born to anything of today. Yet I'd touched the clothes he'd worn on that stormy day, and time had faded away as I experienced *Elaine's* memories and recognized those clothes. What happened to time if you had lived before as a different person and now had her memories as well as your own?

It was as if the past had caught up with me to tell me something. It was my task now to find out what it was I should learn from it.

I concentrated on the diaries, flipping slowly through them.

Elaine had been a tireless diarist, writing almost every day, recording not only the events of her own life but also what was going on in the town, as well as the world in general. I stopped every now and then to read how she felt about a historical event. Like, on November 22, 1963, she wrote, *"I feel as if a light has gone out. The world is less bright, now that John F. Kennedy is dead."*

It hadn't yet become a historical event on the day she made that diary entry. It had been *now*. She didn't know then all I knew about that day, even though I hadn't been there. She had been *experiencing* the pain of the day when she wrote in her diary. She didn't know who had been the assassin, or whether he would be caught, or what would happen to the rest of JFK's family after his death. She didn't know that thirty-six years later the little boy who had saluted his father's coffin would die in a plane crash in the ocean.

I knew all those things.

But what if I could strip away all that I knew and compress time to go back and *be* Elaine on a particular day? Relive an experience? Of course the experience I was thinking of would be painful to relive. I wasn't sure I even had the courage to try it.

And how would I go about doing it, anyway?

I tried to dodge the answer to that one, but I knew what I'd have to do, and it involved going to see Perla Goudy and having her regress me to that day.

Even thinking about it made my heart thump. I was afraid of Perla Goudy.

Or was it *Elaine* who was afraid of Perla?

Quickly I flipped through several diaries, checking for mentions of Perla. I looked for the memory I'd had earlier that day of Perla with Jonathan and Keith, saying, "Isn't this perfect, just the three of us?"

But I couldn't find any reference to it. Apparently Elaine hadn't thought it important enough to write about.

Elaine did talk about Perla every now and then, sometimes relating something they had done together and sometimes expressing exasperation at Perla's odd ways. Perhaps she hadn't even realized that Perla was after Jonathan.

Or maybe I was mistaken about Perla, because I found a passage that told about receiving an announcement of her marriage to somebody named Brett Goudy. Then, in the diary from the following year, I found a card from Perla stuck in the pages, telling of the birth of a son, named Adam.

I didn't find a single thing in Elaine's diaries that would cast any suspicion on Perla. So apparently my feelings of dislike came from me and not from Elaine.

So why not let Perla help in the quest to find out if Keith was alive?

Mom would be coming home from the hospital tomorrow. I'd tell her to go ahead and invite Perla over to our house, as she'd suggested.

No. It would be better to have Perla do her thing without Mom there. What if Perla regressed me and I, as Elaine, saw Keith drown? Could Mom handle that?

Much as I resisted the idea, I knew the best thing to do was to go to Perla's house that very night and see if we could find out anything. Maybe I'd even have good news to tell Mom.

I looked in the telephone book for a listing for Perla. But either she had an unlisted number or else she didn't have a telephone at the cabin, which was likely the case since she spent most of her time elsewhere.

She'd said I could come over anytime. So I would. It was still before nine o'clock. Not too late. But before I did, I read Elaine's last entry in her final diary, the day before she died.

"Made brownies for tomorrow," she'd written. *"Should be a lot of people at the lake to celebrate the completion of the dam and the flooding of the old town site ten years ago. Has it really been that long?"*

Nothing of interest there. Certainly Elaine hadn't had any premonitions of her death the next day.

After closing the diary, I threw on a light sweater and set off for Perla's cabin, around the south arm of the lake. Since the full moon was bright, I decided to cut across the dry end of the lake, walking down an avenue between dried willows, where a street used to be.

Thick dust puffed up around my ankles with every step, but I kept going, knowing this route would shorten my journey by half. The mountains in the background were shadowed, and the shrunken lake glinted like a black diamond in the distance. But my flashlight made a bright tunnel in the darkness so there was nothing to be afraid of. Hadn't I walked these streets before in my life as Elaine? They should be familiar and safe.

A slight breeze sprang up when I was halfway across the dry area of the lake. It rattled the withered willow sticks, making them clack like the dead tongues of old ghosts, telling me to hurry, hurry, hurry out of there.

But that was just my imagination. I'd never been afraid of the dark. Not Carlene. I suspected not Elaine, either. I tried to concentrate on the good times that had happened here before the town was flooded—when Elaine was young. Where had the ice cream parlor been? How about the library, before it was moved? Where were Elaine's memories when I needed them?

I was passing the foundation of the old school when I heard the sound. Like somebody quietly sobbing.

I turned to run back through the thick dust and the clacking willows. But before I could take a step, somebody rose up from the old church foundation. I jabbed my flashlight in that direction, but the beam wasn't quite powerful enough.

"Don't be afraid," a voice said. "I'm glad you're here, Elaine."

seventeen

I was walking down the dark street of the old Lake Isadora, before the town was moved and the area flooded. I'd come to the school to meet my husband, Jonathan, who was the high school science teacher. I'd taught English there for a while, but had recently resigned, now that I was expecting a baby.

There was a light in the science and math room upstairs, and I could see Jonathan's head as he moved about.

Then I heard the sobbing, the only sound in the quiet night except for faint voices coming from the direction of the hotel.

Startled, I froze. Peering into the darkness, I saw a figure hunched on the bench under the old apple tree. The figure rose.

"Don't be afraid," a blurred female voice said. "I'm glad you're here, Elaine."

When I didn't move, she said, "It's Perla."

"Perla?" Now I recognized the voice, distorted from

crying. "I didn't know you were in town, Perla. Whatever's the matter?"

She launched herself at me then, throwing her arms around me and clinging. "Oh, Elaine, Brett's gone." She began crying again.

"Brett?" I repeated. "Gone?" Awkwardly I patted her back.

Perla and I had never really been friends. I'd been sure she was after Jonathan when we were younger. After he and I were married, she'd left town, tired, she'd said, of living alone in the lakeside cabin she'd inherited when her parents died. The next year we'd received an announcement of her marriage to someone named Brett Goudy, and the year after that there'd been a card telling of the birth of a son named Adam. As far as I knew, she'd never come back to Lake Isadora. Until now.

After sobbing on my shoulder for a minute or two, Perla loosed her hold to pull a hankie from the pocket of her skirt. "Sorry," she said. Scrubbing the hankie across her eyes, she gestured toward the bench. "Can you sit down for a few minutes, Elaine? I need to talk."

I glanced briefly up at the lighted window, wishing I could signal Jonathan that I was there. But he'd be coming downstairs anyway in just a couple of minutes to unlock the door for me. We'd arranged beforehand that I would be there at 8:45 and he'd come down to let me in.

"Sure, Perla," I said. "I have time." I followed her to the bench under the apple tree and sat down.

155

She took in a deep breath. "Brett moved out," she said. "Didn't give any reason, except that he doesn't want to be married anymore. Not to me, anyway." She blew her nose in the hankie. "You know how much I love him."

No, I didn't know how much she loved him. I'd never met him nor even seen him.

But I didn't say that. Reaching over to take her hand, I said, "Perla, I'm so sorry."

I didn't know what else to say.

She broke into fresh sobs, wetting my shoulder with her tears again.

I made soothing noises until the crying lessened in intensity. Then I said, "So you and Adam have come back to live in your cabin?"

She didn't say anything, and I wondered if I'd got the name wrong. "Isn't that your little boy's name? Adam?"

Nodding, she straightened her shoulders, seeming determined to get control of herself. But her voice was shaky as she said, "That's the worst part. Brett won't let me take Adam away from Tehachapi. He has him every other week."

"So I guess you're going right back up there," I said limply.

She snuffled back her tears, like a little kid. "Yes," she said. "I just came down for some of my stuff. Brett sold our house and I'm in an apartment now." She smiled at me. "I wish I could stay here among my friends. I'm glad you're still here, Elaine. You and Jonathan."

I heard the rattle of a key in the lock of the schoolhouse door.

Perla tensed. "What's that?"

I let go of her hand and stood up. "Just Jonathan, opening the door. He's been doing some work in the science room."

Perla stood up, too. "Oh!" she said. "I don't want him to see me like this."

To tell the absolute truth, I didn't want him to see her at all. It almost seemed as if she'd been waiting for him there. Waiting, and setting the trap with her sobbing. But that was a mean thought when she was in such pain. So I put a hand on her arm. "Don't go," I said. "You shouldn't be alone right now."

"I'm glad you're here, Carlene," Perla said.

Carlene?

The schoolhouse was gone, and the voices from the hotel. The only sound was the dry clacking of the willows lining the vanished streets.

But Perla was still there. An older Perla than the one in my memory.

"Perla," I whispered. It was all I could get from the desert that was my throat.

In the glow of my flashlight I could see that she raised her eyebrows.

"You remember me?" she said. "I met you so briefly there at the hospital that I didn't think you would."

I remembered her from another life. I thought about

keeping that fact from her. But she knew all about the flashes of Elaine's memories that I'd been experiencing. Mom had told her, in the hopes that she could help me access more of them.

"Elaine remembers you," I said.

The words were no sooner out of my mouth than I wished I hadn't said them. I needed to think about why Elaine had come out so strong when I'd seen Perla there by the foundation of the old school. She may have been trying to tell me something about Perla. But what? That Perla's husband had left her? I'd already known that. Jonathan had told me. Or had it been Mom?

Or was it Elaine?

Perla didn't seem surprised at what I'd said. She came forward, smiling at me in the moonlight. "I'm glad she hasn't forgotten me," she said. "Elaine was a dear friend."

That wasn't quite what Elaine's memories seemed to indicate. But perhaps they *became* dear friends after Perla's husband dumped her. I'd have to check through Elaine's later diaries.

"Where were you going in the darkness, Carlene?" Perla said. "May I walk with you? I was just sitting here reminiscing. Thinking about the way the town used to be, before the valley was flooded."

Was that why she'd been crying? Or had it only been in Elaine's time that she'd cried? Certainly she didn't look as if she'd been crying. I could see her face quite clearly now, in the moonlight. Her voice was soft and husky, but that seemed to be her natural way of speaking.

I felt disoriented and confused. I didn't know how to sort out all the things that were happening. I wished Mom and I had never come to this place.

But we'd come to find out what had happened to Keith. And I had left our little rented house that night to seek out Perla so she could help me remember what had happened to him.

Well, I'd found her.

"I was looking for you," I said. Again she raised her eyebrows, this time in question.

"I want you to regress me," I said. "Tonight."

Perla's cabin was cozy, in a rough, rustic kind of way. There were three rooms, one large combination kitchen-dining-living room and two bedrooms. The kitchen stove was an old black wood-burning range. The battered sink, complete with drainboard, stood on legs beneath a window that looked out at the pines on the lake's edge. There was a brightly colored braided rug on the floor and a shabby but comfortable sofa as well as a couple of overstuffed chairs and a rocker. Ancient photographs in painted wooden frames decorated most of the walls. A dark glass-fronted cupboard held fragile-looking dishes that Perla said had belonged to her grandmother. A tall, wide bookcase held curios as well as books.

"I like your place," I said as I looked around.

"So do I," she said. "I like to come back to it, but I don't get here often. Sit down, dear. Here, in this chair." She indicated a deep, soft chair across from the old-fashioned rocker positioned alongside a low table. I wondered if this was her official "regression chair."

"I'll just make some hot chocolate," she said. "Sit down and I'll bring it to you."

There was a slight chill in the air as night deepened. "Okay," I said, sitting down in the chair.

Perla fussed about the kitchen, reminding me of my grandmother back in Arletta. Grandma, with her families-are-forever needlepoint hanging in her front hall.

"Did you know Keith?" I asked abruptly.

"Oh my, yes," she said. "He was such a dear little boy. Reminded me of Adam when he was a child." She turned from the stove to look at me. "Adam is my son."

"Yes," I said. "I know. Where does he live?"

"North of here. That's where I live, most of the time."

I almost wished I hadn't agreed to have the hot chocolate. I was nervous about this regression stuff, and I wanted to get into it, get it over with, and go on back to our house where I could decide how much to tell Mom of what went on in the session.

"Perla?"

"Yes?"

"Will I know what I'm saying when you regress me?"

Again she turned to look at me. "Sure, honey. You'll be totally conscious."

"Then how does it work? I mean how do I get back to being Elaine?"

She poured the hot chocolate into two fragile cups from the old cupboard. She handed one to me and sat down in the rocker.

"Are you worried about this, Carlene?" she asked. "We don't have to do it tonight, if you're nervous."

"I want to find out what I can before Mom is released from the hospital," I said. "If I find out something bad—" I stopped, not wanting to even think such a thing.

Perla nodded. "You want to be prepared."

"Yes."

Perla sipped her hot chocolate. "I can't say what Elaine will remember, Carlene, but there's no reason for you to be scared about the process of regression."

"Are you going to hypnotize me?"

"What I'll do is try to get you into a state of total relaxation. That will help Elaine's memories rise to the surface of your mind. Then I'll ask questions that will hopefully lead you to remember what Elaine saw the day Keith disappeared." She smiled reassuringly. "It doesn't hurt, honey. Really."

My cup was warm in my hands, and the chocolate was sweet and comforting. Perla's voice was so soothing that I felt relaxed already. "How long will it take?"

"That all depends on how soon we can reach Elaine and how much she remembers." Perla settled back in her chair. "Let's forget Elaine for a few minutes and talk about you, Carlene. Tell me about your life at home. What are your favorite studies? What do you like to do when you're not in school? Do you have a boyfriend?"

"No boyfriend," I said. But I thought of Luke. And Angelique. Where had they gone on their big date tonight? What were they doing? Was he thinking of me?

Duh! Why should he? I had no claim on him.

Perla smiled. "I think you like somebody, whether you admit it or not. You're a very attractive girl, Carlene. It's all right to dream about a good-looking boy."

I giggled, feeling more relaxed and cheerful than I'd been for several days. Why had I felt uneasy around Perla at the hospital? I couldn't even remember now.

Nor why J.P. would have thought she was like the witch in *Hansel and Gretel* when she took hold of his arm.

I found myself liking her.

Maybe what Elaine had wanted to tell me through the scene I'd replayed earlier had been just this: that I was to trust Perla.

eighteen

I settled back in the big chair, feeling relaxed and just a little drowsy from the warm room, the hot cocoa, and the realization I'd just made that Elaine wanted me to trust Perla. I was more happy and hopeful than I'd been since Mom and I first came to Lake Isadora.

I gazed around Perla's cozy home, wondering if Elaine had ever been there, if she'd ever sat in the chair I now occupied.

There was a picture on the low table, right across from where I sat. Like a school class photograph. Probably high school. Approximately twenty students, I would guess.

"Are you in that picture?" I pointed my cocoa cup at the photo.

"Yes." Perla leaned forward to pick up the picture in its painted wooden frame. "Can you imagine, that's our whole tenth-grade class. The high school wasn't as big then as it is now." She held it out to me. "Let's see if you can tell me who's who."

I swallowed the rest of my cocoa and put down the cup. Taking the photo, I squinted at it in the dim light, focusing on the young faces from more than forty years ago. There was Elaine, right in the front row. I knew because I'd just been looking at pictures of her at Jonathan's house. She smiled out at the world, confident that life was beautiful and would treat her well.

Jonathan was right behind her, his dark hair in a fifties flat-top cut. He was tall and straight and looked as if he might be captain of the basketball team. His appearance was much the same as it had been then, except for the graying of his hair.

Perla was in the front row, dressed in a cheerleader's short skirt and a sweater with a large "LI" on the front. For Lake Isadora, I presumed. Her round face and figure hadn't changed all that much.

I pointed out the three people I knew to Perla.

"Don't you remember Barbara Lewis?" she asked, jabbing a finger at a blond girl. "And Davy Van Dyke? The class bad boy? You can't have forgotten him."

"I never knew any of them," I said.

Perla gave a short laugh. "Of course. You're Carlene, not Elaine. But she knew him. He's in town, you know. He's the one who found your mother when she fell. I wonder what he's doing hanging around here." Then she seemed to shift gears and said, "Well, Carlene, are you ready to start? The regression, I mean?"

I nodded, feeling too mellow to talk anymore. I had a twinge of nervousness, wondering if she was going to have me focus on a swinging gold watch like I'd seen in movies. But she'd said she wasn't going to hypnotize me. Just put me in a relaxed state.

I was already in a relaxed state. In fact, I wondered if I could stay awake.

I held the photograph out to Perla, but she told me to keep it. "Perhaps it might help you get to Elaine," she said.

That made sense. I wasn't sure what triggered Elaine's memories, but I assumed that the more things that reminded me of Elaine, the easier it would be to make the transition from this life to that one.

"Close your eyes," Perla said in a soft, storytelling voice. "Settle back in the chair. It's a recliner, you know."

I found the lever that let the chair lean back. It felt good to hoist my feet up.

"Fine," Perla said. "Now take a deep breath and let it out. Relax your arms and legs. Let all the tensions go. Let them drain away."

I did as she said, smiling a little as I visualized a stream of tensions dripping from my fingers and toes.

"Think of your mind as a chalkboard," Perla went

on. "There is writing all over it. Notes and scribbles and even graffiti. Can you see it, Carlene?"

"Mmm," I said without opening my mouth.

"Erase it," Perla instructed. "Pick up an eraser, and carefully erase every word, every letter, every line."

I pictured an eraser. Mentally, I picked it up and began scrubbing at the chalkboard. *There was a lot to erase, and as I went about it I remembered second grade, when being assigned to clean the chalkboard was a reward for good behavior. It was called a blackboard then. We all wanted to be picked to erase the board at the end of the day, and then go outside and clap the erasers together to get rid of the chalk dust. Mrs. Randall had always given the task to the two children who'd behaved best during the day. I was frequently picked, but Davy Van Dyke never was. Davy Van Dyke was a troublemaker.*

But I didn't know Davy Van Dyke.

Ah, but Elaine did, and I realized I'd made the transition to Elaine's memories without even being aware of it. I was thinking of Davy, who was always in trouble. Who never got to erase the blackboard at the end of the day. He probably had a lot on his board that needed to be scrubbed off by now.

What was I erasing from mine? I tried to see the words and sentences as my hand moved back and forth, back and forth. But the eraser was too fast. The words disappeared before I could read them. There was something important written on the board. Something I needed to know. But the eraser kept moving back and forth, and then the board was blank.

"Is it all gone now?" Perla asked in a voice scarcely above a whisper. "Is the chalkboard clean?"

I nodded.

"Where are you?" Perla asked.

"Classroom." My tongue felt stiff and I had difficulty saying the word.

"Who else is there?"

Behind closed eyelids, I looked around the classroom. I saw several of the faces from the picture. "Jonathan," I said, my voice feathery in my ears. "Alice. Bob. Perla. Marie. Davy."

"What class is it, Elaine?"

I looked at the teacher. Mr. Forsgren. "American Studies."

"What's happening?" Perla asked.

"We're taking a test. All but Davy."

"What's Davy doing?"

"He's drawing a picture. He hates tests. He hates school."

"What kind of picture is he drawing?"

I craned my neck to see. "I can't tell. Something dark. Lots of heavy black lines."

"Anything else happening?"

I looked around the classroom. "Jonathan is smiling

at me," I said. "He's waggling his eyebrows and rolling his eyes. Means the test is hard. Perla is watching."

"Let's go to another time," Perla suggested. "What would you like to remember next, Elaine? Graduation?"

I frowned, not quite ready to leave the classroom.

"What do you remember about graduation?" Perla persisted.

Then I was in the small school auditorium, dressed in a cap and gown, walking slowly down the aisle between the rows of proud parents while the tinny piano played "Pomp and Circumstance."

"It was good," I said. "Jonathan was valedictorian. I gave the class prophecy."

"What did you say in the prophecy?"

I smiled, remembering. "That Jonathan would be the scientist who'd design the first spaceship to go to the moon. That Barbara would be the first woman president of the United States. That Perla would be personal psychic to the stars. Movie stars, I meant."

"What about Davy?"

I frowned again. "They wouldn't let me give a prophecy about him. He didn't graduate."

"What happened to him, Elaine?"

Why was she pushing me to remember Davy? Did she *know* something about him, or was she trying to find out something? I fast-forwarded the years. "I don't know. I didn't ever see him again."

"Never?"

I shifted nervously. "Yes. Yes, I did. Once."

"When was that?"

When was it? As I tried to pull up a memory, my heart began to thud. My hands felt sweaty.

"I don't know," I said.

"Yes, you do, Elaine. Think now. When did you see Davy again? Davy Van Dyke?"

I wished she'd stop asking me. I squirmed around in the chair. "I don't know. I can't remember."

"Yes, you can, Elaine. Take it slow. Breathe deeply. Remember when you next saw Davy Van Dyke."

"He was there," I said.

"Where?"

I could feel my face bunch up into a frown.

"Where did you see Davy?" the soft voice insisted. "Where, Elaine?"

The memory was there but the edges were blurry, like when a movie projector is out of focus.

"I don't know," I whispered.

"Think about it, Elaine," Perla said.

I couldn't think. I wanted to sleep. I wanted to shut out the insistent voice.

"Elaine?" the soft voice coaxed.

But I wasn't Elaine. I was Carlene, and I was cramped from sitting still for so long.

My eyes were impossibly heavy, but I dragged them

open. "I'm tired, Perla," I said. "I guess that's all for tonight."

I closed off any thoughts about Davy. What did he have to do with me? I'd wondered once if he'd hurt my mom, there on the rocks by Perla's place. But that wouldn't be bothering Elaine. She wouldn't know about that. Well then, did he have something to do with Keith?

In the flickering candlelight (When had she lit candles?) I saw Perla gaze at me for a moment before she said, "Okay, dear. We'll get back to it another time."

I released the lever on the recliner and sat up straight, feeling as if I were pushing against a wall. I didn't want to even think about the memories we'd brought up. "Can we do it soon? My mom comes home from the hospital tomorrow. I was hoping to find out what Elaine knows about my brother before that."

Perla got up and put out a hand to help me from the chair. "What time is your mother to be released?"

I thought. "They said about noon."

"Come here in the morning," Perla said. "As soon as you get up. We'll try again." She started for the door. "As for now, I'm going to drive you home and see that you're safely tucked into bed."

Safely? Of course I'd be safe. This wasn't Los Angeles or Chicago. But I didn't mind that Perla drove me home. It was past eleven, and the moon was gone. The

171

mountains were dark, and I didn't relish walking past the dusty foundations of the old town that had been under the lake for so many years. Besides, I was a little woozy from my visit to Elaine's memories.

True to her word, Perla accompanied me inside the house and waited until I was ready for bed. "Come as soon as you get up in the morning," she said as she left. "I'll fix breakfast, then we'll do another regression. I feel as if we're about to get to what we want to know."

But did I really want to go there? Elaine was resisting, and from the way my heart had thudded, I was sure we were going to find bad news.

nineteen

Much to my surprise, I slept deeply that night. I had expected to toss and turn, worrying about what would happen the next day, playing every possible scenario, revisiting my worries about Luke and Angelique as well as my nightmares about Keith. Instead, I slept.

I had set my alarm clock so that I'd be sure to wake up early. I wanted to complete the regression before it was time to bring Mom home from the hospital. It wouldn't do to have her there listening when Perla and I—or Perla and *Elaine*—got to the bad stuff I was sure lurked somewhere in Elaine's memory.

When the alarm went off, I was groggy and tired, wanting nothing more than to go back to sleep. A shower helped a little.

After I dried my hair, I looked through Elaine's diaries for references to Davy Van Dyke, other than during their high school years. What had he been to Elaine? Why was she resisting the memories of him on that last day of her life, that day at the lake when Keith disappeared?

I found no mention of Davy, except one that said he was in jail. *Again,* which meant he'd been in jail before. But that was in a diary about ten years after high school graduation.

Well, then, perhaps it was in more recent years that Elaine had had contact with him. Perhaps even on the day of the accident. The day she died. Of course that last day wouldn't be recorded in any diary, but perhaps just before that.

I couldn't find the last diary. I knew I'd brought it home because I'd been reading it before I'd gone to Perla's house. I must have put it down in some odd place. I'd find it later. It was time to go face whatever was to come that day.

Hanging my binoculars around my neck for no reason except that I wanted something familiar with me, I started off for Perla's.

She was bustling about her kitchen when I got there, making toast and putting together an omelet. There was hot chocolate already made, and Perla urged me to sit down and relax with it while she finished cooking.

I took the hot chocolate but didn't sit down. Instead, I stood beside Perla, sipping it and watching her push back the edges of the omelet so that she could turn it over. It smelled good and looked pretty, filled as it was with chopped tomatoes and green peppers and onions. Colorful.

Colorful, like the shirt I'd been wearing that day at the lake. "Confetti-speckled" is what Jonathan called it. "You look great, Elaine," he said, his eyes softening as he looked at me. "You always were the prettiest girl in our class."

I gave him a peck on the cheek. "You're sweet to say that after all these years."

"It's true." Jonathan lifted the picnic basket I'd been packing. There was a celebration that day. It had been ten years since the town had been moved to higher ground so that the river could be dammed and the area flooded. There was to be a program with some skits about the old town and a picnic.

"Speaking of our class," I said, "guess who I saw in town yesterday."

"Perla," Jonathan said. "I talked to her. She's here for the celebration."

I shook my head. "No. The person I saw was Davy Van Dyke."

Jonathan's eyebrows went up. "Davy? Is he out of jail?"

"Yes. This time for good, he hopes."

Jonathan nodded. "I hope so, too. Did he come for the celebration?"

"No." I thought back to what Davy had said. "He was

just passing through on his way to some kind of job with the forest service." I paused. "So Perla's in town, too." I said it casually. I hated to have Jonathan tease me about being jealous of her. But I'd never forgotten how she'd made moves on him before any of us got married. And even afterward.

She was in town only off and on these days. Mostly she lived up north where she could be near her ex-husband and her son who, she said, was in his custody at the moment.

I wished Perla would stay up north all the time.

Jonathan grinned, as if he knew what I was thinking. I think he knew how much Perla wanted him and even liked the idea a little.

"Let's go," I said. "The kids have all gone with their friends, so it's just us."

Our three kids were all teenagers and refused to be seen on such a day with their embarrassing schoolteacher parents.

As we left the "dream house" we were building on top of the hill, I noticed that the day was decidedly gloomy, with a wind sighing down through the canyon where the lake was. Clouds were gathering and there was the scent of rain in the air.

"We'd better go for our boat ride first thing," Jonathan said, "before the water gets too choppy." Rowing a boat out into the middle of the lake was one of our favorite things to do. We headed straight for the little dock just past Perla's cabin, where Jonathan kept our rowboat.

When we got there, we noticed a motorboat with two

people in it already far out on the lake. It tossed rather alarmingly, even though the water at the edge of the lake was fairly calm. The lake was treacherous that way. It was always rougher out there where it was deepest, especially when the wind started blowing down through the canyon.

Jonathan squinted at the boat. "The motor must be dead," he said. "Bad time to lose power."

Whoever it was had probably set out early, when the morning was bright. They'd probably gone out to the little island, which was the top of a small mountain in the middle of the lake. It wasn't the best place to be in a storm, so apparently they'd decided to start for shore. But the motor had stalled, and now they were in peril out there in an uncontrolled boat. Maybe without safety oars.

"I wonder if it's Carl Carter and his boy," Jonathan said. "They keep their boat at this dock, and it's not here."

Keith was only four years old. I prayed it wasn't Carl and Keith out there on the dangerous water.

"Carlene! Carlene!"

I realized that Perla was calling my name. How many times had she said it?

"Carlene," she said again. "Are you asleep standing up?"

I resented her voice. I was getting at what Elaine wanted to tell me without her help. Besides, I wanted that glimpse of my dad, Carl Carter. I hadn't seen him for at least four years. And there was Keith. My brother, whom I'd never known. I wanted to hold on to this scene and call them back from danger. I wanted to prevent what was going to happen.

"Guess so," I said in response to Perla's question. For some reason my tongue felt gross and unwieldy. "Did you want me to do something?"

She glanced my way. "First thing, put down the cup. I don't want you spilling chocolate all over my floor."

The room seemed to tilt a little as I walked over to the counter to set the cup down. I'd finished the hot chocolate, I noticed.

"Okay, now hand me those plates and I'll scoop up the omelet. Let's eat and then get down to business."

I picked up the plates. They seemed heavy, but I grasped them as firmly as I could and took them to the stove. The omelet sizzled gently in the shallow skillet, though suddenly it didn't look so great anymore. My stomach lurched as I smelled it.

I knew I'd have to attempt to eat it after all the trouble she'd gone to, making it.

Perla slid half the omelet onto each plate and added a piece of buttered toast. "Okay," she said, "take them to the table and I'll be right there."

But this time the plates were too heavy for me to lift. I tried to tell Perla, but my mouth wouldn't form the words. All that came out was a grunt.

"Carlene! What's the matter?"

I swayed, reaching for the counter to steady myself. I didn't know what was the matter.

Dropping the spatula, Perla took my arm and guided me to the reclining chair, pushing me gently into it and raising the footrest. "Here," she said. "Lean back. Can you tell me what's wrong?"

I couldn't. My head was spinning. I felt as if I might black out. My arm flew out and knocked a book off the little table next to the chair. It looked like Elaine's final diary. But why did Perla have it?

"Rest for a while, Carlene." Perla's voice came from far, far away.

My eyes closed, and I gave in to whatever was cutting me loose from reality. I was aware that Perla sat down beside me.

"It worked faster than I thought," she muttered, as if to herself. Then softly, coaxingly, she said, "Elaine, are you there?"

I slipped easily back into the scene at the edge of the lake. "Yes." My lips formed the word, but I knew I made no sound.

"Elaine." Perla's soft voice filled my ears. "Elaine, what do you see?"

I saw the tossing boat out there on the lake. I saw Jonathan cupping his hands around his mouth to call to the two people in the boat. "Carl!" he called. "Keith!"

It was much too far for them to hear.

Carl seemed to be fumbling with the motor, trying to start it, we supposed. But the boat continued to drift.

"They're taking on water," Jonathan said. "They're either going to overturn or sink before they can get back to shore."

The wind picked up, ruffling the water into good-sized waves. Rain began to fall as a mountain storm moved swiftly across the lake. The wind howled, and the little boat tossed like a scrap of paper.

Jonathan rushed to the dock where our rowboat was tied. "I'm going out after them," he shouted into the wind.

"I'm going with you," I yelled back. "You'll need me to help."

He didn't argue, and soon we were on our way toward the stricken boat. Jonathan was a powerful rower. Even so, I wondered if we would make it before the motorboat sank.

"Keep them spotted," Jonathan yelled to me above the whine of the wind. "Keep me headed in the right direction."

For countless long minutes we toiled toward the tossing motorboat, seemingly not making any headway at all. We were going to be too late. I looked back toward the shore, hoping to see someone, anyone. But the dock was empty. Even if someone had been there, what could he or she have done? It was up to us.

But when I turned again toward the foundering boat, I saw another motorboat approaching, operated by someone who seemed to know how to handle it on rough water.

"Thank God," I whispered, letting relief wash over me like the waves washed over our boat.

But my relief was premature. As I watched, I saw Carl and Keith's boat overturn.

Then it was as if Elaine fast-forwarded her memories to the most important scene, because she and Jonathan were close to the overturned boat. Keith, crying and obviously terrified, clung to it. Carl was nowhere to be seen.

"Keith," Jonathan called. "Hang on."

The person in the other motorboat was dressed in a yellow slicker and large rain hat. We couldn't see his face, but we cheered when he came close to Keith and pulled him aboard.

"Elaine! Elaine!" It was Perla's voice. "Elaine, tell me what's happening."

"Keith is safe," I said. "He's on the other boat."

"Who saved him?" Perla asked. "Tell me who pulled him from the water."

I gripped the sides of the boat as I peered through the murky air to see Keith's rescuer. But the big yellow hat obscured his face.

"I don't know," I said.

"It's Davy Van Dyke, Elaine," Perla said. "Can't you see that?"

"No," I said. "I can't tell who it is."

"It's Davy Van Dyke," Perla insisted. "Remember that, Elaine. It's Davy."

Jonathan had pulled our boat up close to the motorboat now, as close as we could get on the roiling water.

"We have to find Carl," he yelled to the man in the other boat.

Keith reached out to us, crying and coughing up the water he'd swallowed. "We'll take the boy and go to shore," Jonathan screamed into the wind. "Your boat is heavier. You circle and find Carl."

But instead of pulling closer to us, the motorboat started to move away.

"No," Jonathan yelled. He rowed our boat in front of the motorboat. "Stop! Wait!"

We were very close. I reached out, straining toward Keith. As I did, I saw the face under the yellow hat.

"It was you, Perla," I said through my stiff lips.

I realized even as I spoke that it was the wrong thing to say.

I knew it beyond a doubt when I heard Perla sigh. "Why couldn't you have just accepted that it was Davy Van Dyke, Elaine?" she said. "Everybody knows he's a troublemaker. They would have believed that he took Keith. Now I'll have to get rid of you all over again."

twenty

"Perla," I tried to say. "I'm not Elaine. I'm Carlene. CARLENE!"

But my unmanageable lips and tongue garbled the words. It wouldn't have made much difference anyway. I knew that in Perla's troubled mind I was Elaine.

She grasped my hands and yanked me from the chair, amazingly strong for such a small person. I seemed to have no will. She must have put something in the hot chocolate. Why hadn't I paid more attention to the odd taste? It seemed wimpy of me to have drunk it so obediently.

But I'd had no reason to distrust Perla. My mother had wanted Perla to help us find out what happened to Keith.

Well, now I knew. Or at least I knew that he'd been in Perla's boat just before Elaine drowned. Perhaps she had taken him to be a companion to her own son,

Adam. But that didn't make sense. Adam would have been an adult by the time the accident occurred on the lake. Maybe Adam had already left home and Perla had taken Keith as a replacement. But if that's what happened, where was he now?

My mind slogged along as sluggishly as my feet, but I tried again to form words with my uncooperative mouth. "Where's Keith?" I asked. And again, "Where's Keith?"

"I can't understand what you're saying," Perla muttered.

She towed me out of the cabin and toward the lake. I walked clumsily, unsteadily, unable to resist Perla's strength. My binoculars, hanging as they were around my neck, thumped against my chest.

It was clear what Perla intended to do. She'd drown me, repeating the long-ago death of Elaine. Who would know? I hadn't told anybody where I was going this morning, or even that I'd been at Perla's house the night before.

An old motorboat rocked gently on the water alongside the splintered dock, every now and then giving a friendly nudge to the brightly painted boat drifting beside it. The newer boat I recognized as Jonathan's, the one we'd taken out on the lake.

The boat motors were tipped up and covered. Was the old boat the same one Perla had used the day she took Keith? Elaine would know. But she wasn't giving me any more insights at the moment. Perhaps she had withdrawn completely, terrified of replaying the awful thing that had happened to her eighteen years before.

Perla pushed me toward a weathered bench on the dock. "Sit there," she instructed, shoving me down onto it. "I'll get the boat ready." She went over to take the mooring rope from its post. Swinging her head to look back at me, she said, "We could have avoided this, you know. All you had to do was say *Davy* took that kid. *Davy!* He was here that day. Everybody would have believed you."

Now I knew why Elaine had shied away from thoughts of Davy. Perla had tried to lead me to name him as the person who took Keith, but Elaine knew better.

Perla made a threatening movement, and for a moment I thought she was going to come over and slap me. But then she turned back to the work of getting the boat ready to go.

I thought about running away. There was nothing restraining me. Nothing except that I was frozen like a statue there on the bench, with no will to do anything but sit obediently and watch.

When I heard footsteps, I wondered stupidly if they were my own. But no, I was still seated on the splintery bench.

185

Perla had by now uncovered the motor of the battered boat. As she tipped it down into the water, she looked up.

"J.P.," she said harshly. "What are you doing here?"

J.P., his necktie dangling across his chest as always, came dancing over to plop down beside me on the bench. "Hi, Carlene," he said before greeting Perla. "Jonathan's taking me for a boat ride," he told her. "Luke was too busy, so Jonathan said he'd take me out on the lake today."

Perla twisted her neck to peer back toward the cabin. "Jonathan? Where is he, J.P.?"

J.P. got up and went over to watch what Perla was doing. "He had to go back to the car to get his cell phone. He doesn't want to go out on the lake without it. He'll be here in a minute."

Perla looked at J.P., then at me. She seemed to be considering something. "J.P.," she said in a calm, normal voice. "Why don't you come in my boat with Elaine and me, right now? We'll meet up with Jonathan out on the lake."

J.P. shook his head. "Nah. I'd rather wait for Jonathan." His forehead wrinkled. "Who's Elaine?"

Perla tried to start the motor of her boat. It was the kind where you have to pull a cord really hard. The boat didn't start on the first try.

"We're going to see something special, J.P.," Perla

said as she tried again. This time the engine coughed to a start. "If we go on ahead, we can surprise Jonathan."

Now J.P. was beginning to look uneasy. He glanced at me, slumped and motionless on the bench. He turned to come back to me but before he could, Perla grabbed his arm, yanking him into the boat. He started yelling for Jonathan.

"Elaine," Perla screeched. "Get in the boat!"

"No." My stiff lips formed the word. I couldn't get up to run, but I *could* refuse to get into the boat.

"Elaine! Now!" Perla couldn't leave the boat because J.P. was struggling and screaming.

I heard running feet, and Jonathan came into view. "J.P.," he called. "What's the matter?"

With a venomous look at me, Perla headed the boat out onto the lake, one hand on the tiller and the other trying to control J.P. They were a few yards away from the dock when Jonathan pounded up to me.

"Carlene," he panted. "What's going on?"

My eyes rolled as I tried to speak. For a second I wished it had been Luke who had come. Younger, stronger Luke. But Jonathan seemed to grasp the situation quickly. "Carlene, what has she done to you?" he said, then ran to the end of the dock. "Perla," he yelled. "I'm calling the police."

Pulling his cell phone from his pocket, he came over to help me to my feet. "I'll need your help," he said, half carrying me to the shiny new boat alongside the dock. After seating me quickly, he shoved the phone into my hands, uncovered the motor, and started it.

"Call the police, Carlene," he said urgently.

It was up to me. Jonathan was concentrating on steering the boat in pursuit of Perla and J.P.

Forcing my thoughts to focus, I punched in 9-1-1. Would I be able to speak? My tongue was a stone inside my mouth.

We were gaining on Perla. Her old, cranky boat chugged along at a snail's pace, no match for Jonathan's fast new boat. Apparently hers was leaking, because it now rode lower in the water than it had before.

When the operator came on the line, I gripped the little cell phone tightly and made my mouth say, "Trouble. Lake. Perla's. Come fast."

The operator's firm voice repeated what I'd said. "Can you give me any more information?"

"No," I gasped. "Come."

"Stay on the line," the operator said urgently. "Watch for the rescue boat. Tell me when you see it."

I hoped it would get there in time.

The reassuring voice chattered on in my ear. "Can you tell me what's happening? Are you able to talk?"

To both questions I managed a breathy, "No."

Jonathan and I were right behind Perla's boat now. J.P. stretched his arms toward us.

As I strained toward Keith, the other person in the boat turned and I saw her face.

"Perla," I yelled. "Stop! It's us—Elaine and Jonathan."

Her boat slowed. She stared at us as if she'd never seen us before.

"Where's my dad?" Keith screamed.

In the distance I could see Carl's overturned boat, but there was no sign of him.

"We'll find him," I answered. To Jonathan I said, "Let Perla take Keith to shore. We should go find Carl." I had to shout to be heard over the noise of the wind and water.

Jonathan shook his head as he tried to steady our boat next to Perla's. "Something's going on here," he said. "We have to get Keith."

Suddenly Perla gunned her motor and began moving around us. The choppiness of the water slowed her down, and Jonathan managed to keep our boat alongside. To me he yelled, "Reach for Keith."

We were close enough now for me to touch Keith's fingers again. I wondered if I could lift him from Perla's boat to ours. As I stretched toward him, I lost my balance and fell into the water.

The waves carried me away.

"Hang on!" Jonathan shouted as I dog-paddled frantically. He maneuvered toward me. Perla took the opportunity to gun her motor again and guide her boat away.

"Perla!" Jonathan yelled. "Get Elaine."

Perla looked back at us. Then, to my relief, she turned her boat. But instead of coming to me, she headed toward Jonathan.

"Over there," he hollered, pointing at me. "Get her, Perla."

She shook her head. "Oh, no," she yelled back. "This is perfect, just the three of us."

I'd heard those words before, the day I snapped a photo of her and Jonathan and Keith. The day I realized she wanted to take Jonathan away from me.

This was her chance. She could let me drown and Jonathan would be free.

Jonathan shook his head violently. "Perla, get Elaine!" he commanded.

Her boat was very close to his now. As I watched from the water, Jonathan stood up to reach for Keith. Just then a wave threw Perla's boat against Jonathan's. He lost his balance and fell heavily, striking his head against the side. He disappeared inside the boat and didn't get up.

"Perla," I shrieked. "Come get me. I need to help Jonathan!"

She sat there, staring at Jonathan's boat. Then, as if in slow motion, she turned to look at me. Forcing Keith to sit down, she headed toward me.

"Oh thank you, thank you, Perla," I whispered as I desperately treaded water. I tried to swim toward her, but the waves tossed me in the other direction.

Because of the rough water, Perla had a hard time guid-

ing her boat over to me. But then she was there, pulling right alongside.

Instead of reaching out to me, she picked up an emergency oar from the bottom of her boat and raised it high above her head. As it began to descend toward me, I saw Keith stand up.

The memory ended.

"Oh, Elaine," I whimpered. I couldn't believe Perla would hit her, helpless as she was there in the water. But that's what must have happened. And now I knew the whole story—except where Keith was.

"What's that?" the operator's voice said in my ear. "What did you say?"

I couldn't answer. I couldn't even tell Jonathan to beware. Perla might have an oar in her boat this time, too. Jonathan wouldn't remember that part of what had happened. He had little memory of anything that took place on the lake that day after he fell and hit his head. Was history really going to repeat itself? Everything was in place. I—or Elaine—was in one boat with Jonathan beside me, and Perla was in the other with Keith. No, it was J.P. she had with her. But in her sick mind he was Keith, and she was taking him away again, if indeed that was what she'd done the other time on the lake.

Making a supreme effort I said into the cell phone, "Perla, murderer." Just so somebody would know, in case this replay scene went all wrong, too.

But Perla apparently did not have emergency oars this time. She made no effort to fight us off. In fact, she was staring in horror at her boat, the top of which now rode almost even with the water.

J.P. clutched the side of the boat with one hand. The other was wrapped around his necktie, the ever-present necktie that represented comfort and safety of some kind to him.

As Jonathan brought our boat alongside Perla's, J.P. rose and stretched out his arms again.

But as Jonathan reached for him, Perla grabbed at his legs, and suddenly J.P. was in the water.

I knew he could swim. All the kids in Lake Isadora learned to swim at an early age. But surprise made him flounder, and he began to sink.

"Keith," I screamed. He'd fallen overboard trying to keep Perla from hitting me with the oar. She'd still hit me, but because he deflected the oar a little, it was a glancing blow that stunned me slightly but didn't split my skull. I was still conscious enough to swim toward Keith, yelling at him to stay calm, to let me help him. He was terrified, flailing his arms and choking on the cold water.

"Perla," I yelled, "over here." I had Keith in my arms now. But my head hurt and I was seeing double. Two Perlas stared back at me. Two boats began to pull slowly away from Keith and me.

Keith wrapped both arms around my neck, clinging fiercely. I was losing the battle to stay conscious. I had an overwhelming desire to go to sleep. "It's okay, Keith," I said softly as I looked around for Jonathan. I could see our boat tossing on the waves, but I couldn't get to it. Jonathan must be unconscious. Or dead.

Perla's boat was now several yards away from us, heading toward shore.

"It's okay," I said again to Keith and felt him relax in my arms as we began to sink slowly down, down, down into the water.

twenty-one

I knew this was Elaine's last memory. Now I was back with the problems of my own life. Perla's boat was sinking. J.P. was in the water. Jonathan was trying to maneuver our boat to pick him up. I was still woozy from whatever Perla had put in the cocoa.

I was reaching for J.P. when, without warning, Perla leaped from her foundering boat. She began to sink.

Both Jonathan and I were immobilized by the shock of it, but J.P. paddled quickly over to her. "Perla," he yelled. "Flap your arms."

He was a much better swimmer than Keith had been. Of course, he was three years older. Keith had been so young.

Moving her arms weakly, Perla peered toward J.P. "Adam?" she said softly.

"Give me your hand," J.P. shouted.

When she didn't respond, J.P. took firm hold of her sleeve and tugged her the few feet to the boat.

I was stiff with fear. "Be careful, J.P.," I whispered under my breath. "If she sinks, you could go under, too."

But Perla allowed herself to be pulled to the boat.

When J.P. was close enough, Jonathan seized his hands and lifted him aboard. Fighting hard against the effects of Perla's drug, I reached out for her.

She took the hand I offered. But instead of letting me help her into the boat, she gave me such a hard yank that I was suddenly in the water, too. I tried to swim away, but she grabbed for the binoculars that still hung around my neck.

"Come with me, Elaine." She began to sink, dragging me after her.

The instinct for self-preservation kicked in. I struggled to slip the strap of the binoculars over my head, but Perla had twisted it so that all I did was use up most of my oxygen.

I was Elaine, and I was going to drown again. With me would go the memories of what Perla had done. No one would ever know the truth. Mom would never find out what had happened to Keith.

I felt as if I were looking into my binoculars the wrong way again. From far away I saw Elaine and Keith sink deeper and deeper into the lake. I was watching them drift gracefully with the movement of the water, Keith cradled in Elaine's arms.

Watching. Not *experiencing.* I wasn't Elaine. I was Carlene, and I didn't have to repeat history. I had a mission, to take the sad truth to my mother, to comfort her as best I could. Wasn't that why Elaine's memories had come to me? Even if Mom hated me for being the bearer of the horrible news, I must survive to tell her.

Perla probably assumed I was unconscious. She relaxed her grip on the strap, and that's when I twisted out and away from it, kicking my legs furiously despite my bursting lungs.

I began to rise upward to light. To life.

I was almost to the surface when I felt strong arms around me. Jonathan was there. Together we struggled up to air.

Coughing and sputtering, I clung to him. "I saved you this time, Elaine," he whispered softly.

Had the horror of the last few minutes plunged him back into the past?

But then he said, "So glad you're all right. Stay here with J.P." After he clamped my hands onto the edge of the boat, he followed Perla down into the water. I wondered dully if I wanted him to save her. She deserved to die as Elaine had died.

But then she would escape the consequences of what she'd done all those years ago.

J.P. was patting my hands and murmuring softly. "Hang on, Carlene," he crooned. "The boat is almost here." He pointed out onto the lake.

Far away I saw a boat speeding toward us, and then it was there, a large powerboat carrying men who held rescue equipment at the ready as they swung alongside.

The next several hours are a blur. I remember Luke being on the rescue boat. I remember him wrapping me in a blanket and holding me close, murmuring my name over and over. I heard his voice telling somebody—me, probably—that he'd called the authorities in Tehachapi, trying to find out something about Perla. He'd learned plenty, he said, mainly that there was no husband, although she'd been married very briefly several years before. There had never been a son named Adam.

Then, suspicious about Perla, Luke had gone out looking for me. The emergency call had come in, and he'd talked his way onto the rescue boat.

I could hear myself babbling about someone drowning, which alarmed the rescue team. "Keith," I repeated over and over. I heard Jonathan assuring the rescuers that we were all accounted for—himself, J.P., a limp Perla, and me. He said Keith had drowned a long time ago.

Keith had drowned. Little blond, sweet-faced Keith who had relaxed trustingly in my arms as we'd drifted down through the water.

No, not *my* arms. *Elaine's* arms.

They gave me some kind of shot at the hospital. I woke later to find Mom, her head still swathed in bandages, holding my hand. Jonathan stood at the foot of the bed. No, it was Luke. He looked so much like Jonathan when he'd been young. When Elaine and he had been young.

"Carlene," Mom said anxiously. "Are you all right?"

My head seemed clearer now. "I think so." I looked around. "Where's J.P.?"

Luke grinned. "He and Grandpa went to the cafeteria for hot dogs. J.P. said he was starving."

Relief washed over me. "Then he's okay."

"Hot-dog okay," Luke said. "We're all okay. I even have your binoculars. Perla still had hold of the strap when Grandpa brought her up." He walked around the bed to hand them to me. "They got pretty waterlogged, but I cleaned them up for you."

I took them, grateful to feel their solid surface again. "And Perla?" I asked.

Mom and Luke exchanged glances. "Physically, she's all right," Mom said.

I took that to mean she'd gone over the edge

mentally. I wondered if she had the capacity to answer the questions I wanted to scream at her. I'd find out later.

In the meantime, I had something to tell Mom. Stalling for time, I raised the binoculars to my eyes and pointed them toward the window. I could see part of the lake. The powerful lenses brought the water as close as my fingertips, just as Elaine's memories had brought Keith close to me. Keith, my ghost brother whom I'd resented all my life. There was no resentment now, just regret that I had never shared his companionship. But I felt as if I'd known him.

I thought of Grandma's wall hanging. *Families are forever.*

I took a deep breath. "Mom," I said. "I know about Keith."

Her hand tightened around mine as I told her of Elaine's last memory.

"Oh, Carlene," she cried when I'd finished. "My poor, darling Carlene. What a terrible thing for you to go through. Will you be all right?"

She leaned over to hug me, the roughness of her bandages scraping against my cheek. "I'm so very grateful that he wasn't alone," she said.

As she began to weep softly, I realized that her first thought had been of me. Of *me*.

• • •

Perla confessed everything after she recovered from her near-drowning. Although she rambled a lot, the authorities were able to get to the truth. How she'd built a fantasy world around somehow snaring Jonathan and then taking Keith to complete the picture of her perfect family. She'd seen her chance that day on the lake.

But it had all gone wrong, and Keith drowned along with Elaine. She'd never meant for that to happen, she said. It was supposed to be just Elaine. But Keith had seen too much, and she'd decided to let him go, too.

Perla said she'd found Keith's body the night after he'd drowned. He'd washed up on the rocks near her cabin, as if he'd come to her. She'd taken him to the old mine for burial so nobody would see. She'd changed his clothes, dressing him in a little suit she'd bought years before for her fantasy son. She hadn't remembered leaving his little shorts and shirt there in the mine until she'd read in the newspaper about them being found.

It's all so twisted. But it's easier for us to know the truth.

I'll never be able to explain my part in what happened. All I can say is that my experiences with Elaine's memories are sort of like the old town of Lake Isadora. If you didn't know the history of the area, you'd never realize the town had once been where the lake is now. But when the drought lowered the water level, the fragments of a previous life were revealed.

Mariah firmly maintains that I lived a previous life as Elaine. She says that some things are so important they will come out in whatever way is possible, like water seeping through a crack in the rock face of a mountain.

We did what was necessary for Keith, moving him to the pretty cemetery on the bank of the lake.

We've never located Dad to tell him the whole story. Maybe it doesn't matter, since he always believed Keith was dead.

Mom and I continue to heal. I know now that she loves me. We've decided to live permanently in Lake Isadora. J.P. practically lives with us when he's not in school. His aunt Fran understands. Luke practically lives with us, too, though he's more like a big brother to me than anything else. He and J.P. act like brothers, and sometimes I see them both as Keith, as a child and as a young adult. It's confusing and will take time to sort through.

But we function like a family as we try to untangle the snarled threads of our lives.

J.P. must have untangled something. He still mentions his mom and dad occasionally, but one day he folded his battered necktie into a small box and buried it.

I think of that necktie now and then. It has become a symbol to me of the link between the past and the present, the bond between human beings, whether blood-related or not. A reminder that families are indeed forever.